MEANING

FOR

WIFE

A MEANING FOR WIFE

MARK YAKICH

BROOKLYN, NEW YORK

"Vertigo" from *Poems 1955-2005* (Bloodaxe Books, 2005) by Anne
Stevenson, copyright© 2005. Used by permission.

Printed in the United States of America
10 9 8 7 6 5 4 3 2 1

Ig Publishing
392 Clinton Avenue
Brooklyn, NY 11238
www.igpub.com

Cover design: Sohrab Habibion

Library of Congress Cataloging-in-Publication Data

Yakich, Mark.
A meaning for wife / Mark Yakich.
    p. cm.
ISBN 978-1-935439-41-7
1. Single parents--Fiction. 2. Bereavement--Fiction. 3. Adult
children of aging parents--Fiction. 4. Domestic fiction. I. Title.
PS3625.A38M43 2011
813'.6--dc22
                            2011030466

For A.
(1977 – 2007)

Strictly speaking, we do not make decisions, decisions make us.
—*All the Names*

1.

Instead of where you are, imagine you're at home sitting on the couch or in your office chair. This could be New York or New Orleans or New Delhi. In any case, try not to be so damn anxious. You're still on Earth, aren't you? But who is this you who is and isn't you?

Oh Christ, calm down. Despite feeling out of character and more worried than usual, take a breath. In order to keep moving, to keep doing the things you're supposed to be doing, you're going to have to give yourself orders, imperatives.

Take a deeper breath and begin again with what your senses tell you.

The seat is uncomfortable, true, but you are warm and safe inside this shell. The plane is still on the ground.

It is a fine day out there for flying. And the aircraft does appear new and the latest in aerodynamic technology. Everything smells right—a mix of fresh black coffee, almond-scented hand soap, and artificial rose disinfectant. You're not going to enjoy the next couple of hours, but it's better than driving cross-country while a toddler alternates between screaming and fidgeting in the backseat. This is no way to travel—without a wife. Then again, you don't have much of a choice.

After tearing off the cover of your magazine and a small

but significant tantrum, your son finally falls asleep after you crush up a Benadryl and slip it into his bottle of orange juice. You know juice is bad for his eleven teeth, but they're only baby teeth and you'll be more careful when he gets older.

You lay him down in the empty seat next to you. Holding his hand, you begin to drift off and in that beautiful state between awake and asleep, you remember childhood insomnia. The only way you could fall asleep was to lie down next to your sister in your parents' bed—because being scared of the dark or the night or a burglar or a house fire or whatever you were scared of, at least you knew that whatever happened you wouldn't be alone. She would have to endure it too. Now with your son sitting next to you on take-off, you feel the same way. If this overgrown metal and plastic bird crashes, at least you'll be together.

You wake up to Owen's pinching your nose with his entire fist. It is not unpleasant. He wants something to eat; you offer him Cheerios, a Granny Smith apple, raisins, mini-bagels, a cheese stick, and half of a tuna fish sandwich. He shakes his head to all of them. To which you reply, "You just don't know what good is," and take a large bite of the sandwich. He says "cha-cha," which means "chocolate." When is he going to start speaking for real? He is almost two years old, and you're a little worried there's a problem. "Cha-cha," he says again. You pretend not to understand and offer him the cheese stick again. He makes a face and then takes it.

It's going to be a long weekend and you're already exhausted.

But you had better rule out one thing first: No sleeping with other men's wives or, for that matter, other men. No reason for this to become a soap opera or a weekend blowout; it is simply a twenty-year high school reunion. Relax. Two decades of forgotten memories or memorable forget-me-nots. Your body may feel different now but as The Professor says, "Mind don't matter and matter don't mind." The Professor (his own moniker) teaches psychology at Tulane and specializes in why people commit suicide—but what the hell does he know, all day he admires the minds of coeds who wear bikini tops and no underwear to class. You've known The Professor since grad school and right now, despite his flaws or maybe your own, you should listen to an old friend.

Owen is well occupied with your headphones, the mini TV screen in front of him, and the chocolate bar he haggled from you. You take out the book you brought. It's been billed as the new Great American Novel. A colleague suggested it to you as a replacement for *The Catcher in the Rye* for your Senior English class. You open it up and begin reading, but after a couple of pages you lose concentration. It's probably not the book's fault, you're simply not in the mood for earnestness and depth.

Instead you look back over the reunion details. Julia, one of your closest friends in high school, and Jackie, the senior class president, set up a website. They scanned in everyone's senior picture from the yearbook. Class members could post information about themselves—where they live, name of their partner, occupation, children, etc. Out of 352 class members, 241 posted information on the website and 127 RSVPed that they would attend the reunion. You know the exact numbers because you've been checking the website everyday for months, even downloading most of the pages to your laptop. It's a pathetic but vital distraction.

You click "Classmate Profiles" and still can't get over how immediately recognizable these names are, how most of their faces, and their whole bodies (at age 18) pop into your mind without any trouble. Take your old friend and class valedictorian Carmen Newberry's entry:

> After graduating from Michigan State, I worked in Detroit for a couple of years and then moved to Florida. I met my husband in 1993 and we married in 1999. We have one beautiful daughter (Fiona, 2) who we cherish. We own a barbecue restaurant (primarily takeout) that my husband runs. Life is good—we are blessed.

The English teacher in you examines this closely: Why did she include "who we cherish"? Don't all parents cherish their little whelps? And why the parenthetical "primarily takeout"? Is that supposed to make more modest the success of the family business? You can't help to notice the overall concision of the entry. Is there any correlation between the length of an entry on the "update" and a classmate's current state of happiness? The more words a person uses to describe what's happened to him or her since high school, the more happy he or she is? Or do fewer words constitute less of an effort to embellish and therefore translate into greater happiness? How many words does it take to become totally happy?

At least you hope Carmen is happy now. Despite her 4.0 GPA, she certainly wasn't happy in high school. Not that you didn't like her—you did—she was part of your clique and taught you the meaning of wit and sharp sarcasm and, come to think of it, cynicism too. Which is perhaps why it took you a couple of months to post something on the website—so people didn't think you were unreachable, unapproachable or, worse, dead. You posted your email address and one of your favorite photos of you and your son. The picture is almost a year old but it's a happy one. You are in a swimming pool and he is lying on an inner tube with his index finger pointing up at the sky. You're looking at him in admiration: After teaching him for months to look at the billowy clouds, he's finally seen his first animal. "Rahhhr," he growls, and not even bothering to look up, you tell him you see the lion too. The smile on his face is a horizon line you could walk along forever. At least that's what you said to your wife when she printed the first copy of the photo. She was always taking and printing photos, and would stay up for hours, downloading, retouching, cropping, printing, and then indexing them into albums. It became her obsession (you made the tally just last month: 13 albums of printed photos; 5,738 digital images; 16 videos) and this obsession took away time you and she might have spent together after Owen went to bed each evening. She, downstairs with the computer and printer; you, upstairs with your laptop, sometimes grading papers, sometimes looking at porn. You could have been talking about your day, about things other than Owen, or you could have been making love. Now of course it's bittersweet—you're glad you have the photos to spark memories, but they also are place markers for the time that is now no time.

The plane hums along punctuated every so often by turbulence. Instead of clutching the armrests, you've learned over the years that it's better to wedge the tops of your shoes underneath the supports of the seat in front of you; this attracts less attention from fellow passengers. It's irrational of course: everyone knows that a plane nearly never goes down mid-flight. But then you recall that one Korean airliner accident you read about years ago where part of the plane's body suddenly ripped off at 35,000 feet and eight passengers were sucked into the engine.

Everything is fine until there's a loud thud followed by a knocking sound. You look around. One of the beverage carts has lost a shelf.

But then the "Fasten Seatbelt" sign lights up, and it grows dark gray outside the windows. The plane banks hard left, right, and then dips. Nobody else seems to notice. Then another shake. You can feel and hear the plane adjust its speed and direction, back and forth as if it's trying to outmaneuver God. Do you even believe in God? If not, then who are you always talking to?

You tear out a blank page from your book. With a felt-tip pen, you draw little squiggle heads for twenty or thirty minutes until the plane finds smooth air. The whole time Owen has been enraptured by the TV. You never used to let him watch a lot of TV. Oh well, things change. Planes crash. People die. You open up the laptop and realize after a couple of minutes that you're staring and not blinking. Things certainly change. Sleep deprivation, constant colds, etc. You begin seeing faces in the computer screen. Not in the actual photos of your classmates, but there in the spots of the screen where there are minute scratches and scrims of dust. Is that face Alex Mueller's, you wonder? Of course you're doing a lot of wondering these days. You hate the phrase "these days" but what else are you supposed to call them—nowadays? post-wife days? Daze. You wonder, what if you'd taken the Alex Mueller route—stayed in Europe as an expat, not come back to the States for grad school. There was that option a decade ago to go to Slovenia, maybe even find some distant relatives, with the Peace Corps. You could have been of some use to someone somewhere, not merely another middle-class suburban kid who has done some grad work. At least in Europe you could have married a European, gained access to all those countries, and your kids could have had European Union passports. So now each time you look at that yearbook photo of Alex Mueller (and apparently even in the dust motes), you think of the women of the European Union, the might-have-beens, and of one particular Irish-Spanish lass, a petite, fair-skinned,

jet-black haired, and naked Camino O'Reilly who once performed less-than-dazzling fellatio on you on the floor of your
flat in Brussels on a random Tuesday afternoon. Alex Mueller—
though probably once would have given you a decent blow-
job—now stands in for passports of many kinds.

Late one night last week, you got on the computer with the
idea of updating your profile. Under "Hobbies & Interests," you
typed "European women, monster trucks, Buddhist meditation,
and bukkake." You were only fooling around and maybe a little
drunk, but a large part of you wanted to click Submit. You are
and you are not the same person you were in high school, and
there is no way you could relate this on a fucking website.

How would you relate, for example, the story of your
mother-in-law? The first time your wife (then girlfriend) told
you about her mother (Little Ma) and her mother's fourteen-
year struggle with colon cancer, you started taking notes on the
meaty part of your hand: *Her entire adult life has been under the shad-
ow of mother's cancer.* This was during your writerly phase. In any
case, your-wife-to-be became irate, called you an incorrigible
ass, and stewed for a couple of days. The next time you started taking notes she just called you obnoxious. People can get
used to anything—as is evidenced by the great donut hunt. You
can't look at a donut anymore without thinking about dying.
Little Ma couldn't eat anything but sweets by a certain point in
her disease, and a glazed chocolate donut was required. Little
Ma, your wife, and you combed the city for just such a donut.
The only two Dunkin' Donuts were sold out, and there were
other donut shops but no glazed chocolate. The last chance was
the largest grocery store in the area. Surely, they would have
a fine Saturday evening selection of donuts in preparation for
the early Sunday morning donut stampede—the rush of young
husbands buying their young wives Sunday newspapers, nonfat

yogurt, low-carb croissants, and egg whites, and French crullers for themselves to eat on the way home.

When the three of you arrived at the store, you were certain that you'd find the donut before they would. This would make you appear useful, even valuable. *Husband Locates Elusive Donut, Saves Woman From Grave Disease.* Pushing on ahead of them, knocking down a small child and a stand of cherry, pumpkin, and mincemeat pies, you turned a corner and there they were—two stalls of donuts. One on the right and one of the left, but which one do you search first? By pure instinct you headed left—plain, powdered white, blueberry filled, donut holes, éclair-like gooey things—but no chocolate. You stopped an employee. *What kind of stock is this? I know there are others, where are they?* You shook him by the shoulders. *You're going to tell me!* He fessed up: Aisle 9, right side, all the way at the end. You ran, zipping past the hordes, in and out, cutting back and forth like a champion skier. Amazing because you'd never skied before. There was an intricate spin move you were thinking of trying, between an old lady and her husband who was bent over comparing cans of corn—but no, *Don't be a goddamn fool,* you said to yourself, *It's too risky.* You headed down Aisle 8 because it had lighter traffic, only a young couple strolling hand-in-hand, you zoomed by full-tilt, unnoticed. But in order to manage, with any kind of efficiency, the hairpin turn around the end of Aisle 8 into Aisle 9, you were going to have to grab on to something. There was a large man who might just be able to help. Yes, he was fat enough. And that long mantel he was wearing would probably withstand the centrifugal force. It was either him or a kiosk of new sparkling wines—not even a close decision. The man didn't perceive at first that he was being of great use to you, but you got hold of his pant leg instead of his coat sleeve, as you'd planned, and you pulled around the end of the aisle, tucking right leg underneath in slide-tackle position, right shin and left hamstring burning along the polished cement floor, you completed the hairpin, and as if in afterthought the fat man screamed as if he were on fire. No matter. You saw them. They were chocolate and they were glazed. You clutched two boxes of twelve to your chest and ran back to find Little Ma and your wife. They were in the cookie aisle, contemplating a package of vanilla wafers. "Here," you gasped, "look what I happened to find." You stuck out the slightly crushed boxes. Little Ma took one in her hands and studied it. "These are frosted." "What?" you said. "I don't want these," she said, "there're no glazed?" She handed the box back to you. "But they looked glazed," you said. "They're not," your wife-to-be said. In the end, Little Ma decided to go with some kind of marshmallow cookie, called a Mallomar, which you'd never tried and never plan to.

2.

After the usual snafus with luggage at O'Hare, you and your son are standing on a curb. It's Friday rush hour and a logjam. Your father is making the pickup. In the old days when you visited home after many months, he'd come inside and meet you right off the plane at the gate; but now security and fear have turned everything into curbside pickup. This would be fine if he or Mom had a cell phone. Their car is a dull beige sedan and always gets camouflaged in the pack, especially on this gray evening; this is going to be a real hunt.

Owen is motioning and moaning in the direction of a very large man with a muzzled dog. "Just a sec, hon," you say, looking for something to distract him. From your shirt pocket you hand him a crumpled boarding pass, "Go for it." He may eat it but, like sitting too close to the TV, you can allow it once in a while. Just don't let these things become habits.

Habits. Six months ago you decided to break a few of them. To do things differently than before, to forge new patterns. It was kind of your own personal addition to the famous Kübler-Ross stages of grief. You started with small things—brushing teeth with the left hand, changing shampoo, drinking green tea instead of coffee. If you started with the small things, you figured at some point you could change the big things. Move to a new apartment, for example.

None of it did much for your mental state, so you made a modification to your new stage of grief—don't break patterns, instead break things. One night you scooped Owen out of his bed, stuffed him tenderly into the car seat, and started driving. You didn't know where you were headed exactly, just somewhere remote. The bayous. Owen wouldn't settle down in his seat; he knew something was up. He kept wiggling and making mouth-fart noises, something cute you'd taught him long ago, which your wife hadn't approved of and which was now nerve-wracking.

You turned on some classical music and rolled down the windows. The hot spring winds replaced the air conditioning and after ten minutes the boy fell back asleep. But you couldn't wait to get to the bayou. The next turn-off would have to do. Down an unlit one-lane road to nowhere, you began throwing them out the window, one by one, yelling *Goodbye and Good Luck! Fuck you, Good China! Fuck you Beijing, fuck you Shanghai!* You expected each dish and glass to sound with a violent crash. But of course they didn't. You were driving too fast and by the time they hit the ground the sound was carried backward. No pleasure even in breaking shit. And now you'd have nothing to eat on tomorrow, having donated the regular dishes to the Salvation Army weeks earlier. Alas, you weren't very good at grief six months ago and you're not much better at it now. *You have a lot to learn,* as your mother said periodically to you as a child. Of course you always knew there was sarcasm in that statement, but now you believe there's an earnest reminder in there as well.

It only takes an hour and a few more papery things for Owen to chew on, including inserts from your magazine, to find the right beige vehicle. You make a mental note to ask the pediatrician about this paper eating—what's the name for the disease, picca?

Dad greets you with a smile and a handshake and gives Owen a little pat. "Hello there, little man." You pile into the car just ahead of a police car blaring its sirens.

The ride home will be forty-five minutes, if you're lucky. You could really use a nap, a coffee, and a shot of bourbon, in that order.

"What classes are you teaching this fall?"

Dad always asks the same question, and you're not sure if he ever hears the answer. If he asks other questions, they're not really questions—they're excuses for him to talk about the latest paranoia sweeping the country or the world. A few years back, before Owen, when you and your wife took a vacation to Europe, he continually warned you about Algerian muggers in Paris. *Don't go out at night, those terrorists will take your passport and you'll never be able to come back.* Last year it was red grapes from Chile purposefully laced with salmonella.

"I said, what are you teaching this fall?"

"Sorry, I'm a bit wiped out. Research Methods, Senior English, and The Novel."

"How do you teach novels on the computer?"

Dad has never really understood your job as a teacher in a virtual high school. You don't blame him. Sometimes you think the job is ridiculous, too, teaching English online to mostly home-schoolers and prisoners. But when you dropped out of the doctoral program with only a master's, you knew a college teaching gig was out of the question. And you could never go back to a cube in an office, unless the job came with a suicide clause.

After an involved explanation of email, websites, and blogging, you notice that Owen is asleep again. Is he getting too much sleep? Is he depressed? Is that possible for a two-year-old?

Fortunately, Dad is an extreme introvert and won't say

much for the rest of the ride home. You do wish you could talk to him about real things. In the twenty years since you left home, only coming back for holiday visits, he has never phoned you. You have called home and Mom has called you. But not once has Dad called you, independent of your mother, not even after your wife died.

You figure it's just his way. Your parents have always been eccentric, though not in a way that's really ever interested you. They may have believed in holistic medicine, acupuncture, and vitamin supplements long before such things gained mainstream popularity, particularly in the Midwest, but as they've aged they've gotten increasingly judgmental and seem to have strong, if not vehement, opinions about everything. The last time you called home, for example, your mother kept going on and on about how there's a cure for cancer but the American Medical Association keeps it under wraps. As gently as you could you tried to interject that that would require an impossible conspiracy between thousands of doctors, medical schools, drug companies, as well as every branch of government. But she argued that it was possible, and that's when Dad added *If they can cover up Roswell, they can cover up anything.* Your parents aren't total conspiracy-heads, however. They do believe we walked on the moon, if only because your father worked for the Raytheon Corporation and led the engineering team that developed Apollo 13's guidance system.

You're almost home when Dad says, "When's this reunion of yours?"

"Some people are meeting at the football game tonight, but the actual event is tomorrow night." You tell him this, but you're still undecided about going. Part of you believes that Owen has been long overdue for a visit to grandma and grandpa's and the reunion was simply a good excuse for a visit. Maybe you should move back to Chicagoland, to be closer to them and your sister. None of them seems overly eager to visit you in New Orleans. Dad would fly, but Mom hasn't been on a plane since she was thirty. You've suggested the train, but she says it's too expensive. They've threatened to drive a few times but her office manager job always seems to get in the way. *Too busy—that OGO conference I have to organize is a bear, Dr. Janis wants all these transcripts by Monday, I have all the fellowship applicants to review, etc.* It is plain to you that she knows more about the lives of her boss and office mates than she does about your life, which is probably as much your fault as hers.

You walk in the front door, Mom hugs you and Owen, and you're genuinely glad to see her. She has dinner almost prepared. When you visit, she usually makes one of your favorites. Tonight it's homemade macaroni and cheese, garlic bread, string beans, cucumber and tomato salad, and chocolate pudding pie. It's nice to feel something resembling normality. You set Owen down in the family room, next to a box filled with toys they keep for him and your sister's four-year-old, Pearl. Mom says she'd love to play with Owen while you unpack. Owen is not so sure but you figure he's got to get to know her.

Unpacking uses up only a few minutes, but you take your time afterwards. You are happy to have a moment alone. Sitting on the toilet in the bathroom you and your sister used to share, you look over at the four-foot tall stack of your mother's astrology magazines. Might as well pull one of them out and begin reading; it could be a while. After a couple of minutes reading, something feels funny. You flip to the front cover. The magazine's date is February 1986.

You remember the year well. It was a few days before your

sixteenth birthday when Mom first told you about your father's schizophrenia. She had to; she'd pulled you out of a track meet to go pick him up at his office. He was being fired. On the half-hour car ride, she told you the story, or part of it, beginning with a diagnosis more than ten years earlier. You were more shocked by the secrecy than the actual news; you would realize your mistake in the following months. Things changed: Dad underwent expensive and ineffective homeopathic treatments (your parents forgoing traditional medicine after his suicidal reaction to lithium in the early 1970s) believing that a food allergy was making him hear voices; Mom went back to work after sixteen years, as a secretary in another suburb an hour away; and, you and your sister retreated to separate caves.

1986. At first you thought *Why him? Then Why me?* And finally just plain *Why?* It took you a while to figure it out—in college or in your early twenties somewhere—to realize that some kind of terrible thing—mental illness, cancer, starvation, war, genocide, dentures, etc.—happens to everyone if they only live long enough. Until you were sixteen, you were simply in a kind of "non-trauma window," as The Professor calls it.

One more quick glance at your sign's astrological forecast. This one for February 23, 1986: "It's another good day at work. The comments about you are uplifting. Don't be afraid to put your creative self out there in front of everybody." Whatever. You leave the bathroom despite failing to empty your bowels.

Owen and Mom have moved to the kitchen. He is standing on a rickety-looking stool, stirring the macaroni and cheese. He has a big smile on his face and so does your mother. She tells him how his daddy used to be a good helper in the kitchen. You do remember once cooking a piece of steak using every spice in the house and that it was mighty tasty, but you can't remember taking part in any other cooking as a kid. That was always Mom's job until, well, things changed.

Owen finishes his project by dropping the spoon into the pot. It sinks slowly and beautifully. Your father comes in the kitchen. Owen suddenly lunges for you to hold him. Typical stranger anxiety. Your father reaches into a cupboard and says to Owen, "Do you want some pop?" You don't want to cause a fuss, so you let Owen have half a glass.

"Do want some red wine?" Dad says.

This is a recent development. Your father's father was an unacknowledged alcoholic and your mother never let booze in the house while you were growing up, except for your high school graduation party. But last year your father heard about the antioxidant properties of red wine and so now he has a glass or two at dinner. Grateful for something to take the edge off, you accept his offer.

The table gets set and dinner goes pretty well. There's the usual squabbling between your parents about his using too much salt, her not wanting ice cubes in her water, etc. These little reruns don't faze you anymore. Owen is the center of attention anyway. He landscapes his food on the table and then applies it to his face, trying a bit of everything. You aren't that hungry for some reason.

As you're getting up to help clear the table, Dad throws out a new piece of information, "Did you hear that they're outlawing vitamin C in Canada and that it could happen here?

"I don't think they can do that, Dad."

"Oh yes they can," Mom chimes in. "I read it on Alternet. Just because it's not being reported by the mainstream media doesn't mean it's not going to happen."

"It's not a medication," you say, "that'd be like banning garlic."

In the background Owen seems to be enjoying this debate, clapping every few seconds.

"Garlic," Dad says, "has incredible antioxidant powers."

You resist the urge to bring up his mania two summers ago—twenty cloves of raw garlic per day. Somehow Mom put up with three months of it. Somehow Dad's stomach survived.

When you and Owen climb the stairs to your old bedroom, which smells of mothballs and old clothes, you recall part of the problem with coming home: the house itself. Growing up you felt comfortable in this place. And you especially liked your bedroom, arranging and rearranging your furniture every six months or so, imagining one day you'd be an architect. The house was a newly built four-bedroom colonial when your parents bought it, moving back to the Midwest from Boston when you were five. The whole subdivision was new, built on grade-A farmland—you can still remember picking clover-like weeds, hundreds of them, from the backyard so that your parents could lay the sod stacked like firewood in the driveway. But the house is now more than thirty years old, and to say that it's a pigsty doesn't due justice to either "pig" or "sty." Although you remember vividly the intense picking-up and cleaning sessions the night before Thanksgiving and Christmas, you don't recall the house being this bad. In all these years Mom and Dad have never thrown or given anything away. It's 2200-square feet of cat-scratched furniture packed into rooms, closets jammed with hundreds of thrift-store shirts, blouses, sweaters, pants, jackets, and skirts on cheap metal hangers, and assorted piles of papers, household junk, and baubles.

Your mother comes in with fresh linens and begins making up the bed. As he does at home, Owen starts pulling books from the large bookshelf against the far wall. He has become quite skilled: the books, some of them tomes, barely miss his toes.

"Ma, where are my yearbooks?"

"Your what," she says, "I haven't touched a thing."

"Yearbooks—I've always kept them right here," you say pointing to the bottom of the bookshelf. "This corner. Should be at least two or three of them."

She shrugs.

"Dad—"

"Oh don't bother to ask, he doesn't know where anything is."

"You two in a fight?"

"No," she says, and then after a moment, "I wanted him to pick up my blouses at the cleaner's today. And, for once in his life, pick up the house, vacuum. He didn't do a damn thing as usual."

You shrug.

"Come downstairs after Owen goes to bed. Goodnight, sweetie," she says, and gives the little guy a tight squeeze.

After getting him into his pajamas, you read him one of his favorite books. It is about an elephant and a mouse who fall in love against the wishes of their families, and it only takes eight or nine reads before he looks sleepy. You're about to do the final tuck-in when he puts his hand in his mouth twice, which is the sign that he's hungry. But then he pulls at his ears. It could be one of the ear infections he's prone to.

"Do your ears hurt?"

He covers his ears and then throws up his hands. "Eeeeet."

"What's wrong with your ears?"

"Eeeeet," he says and sticks a hand in his mouth.

"We just ate."

One more time with the sign.

Back downstairs. Your father is watching TV and your mother has already fallen asleep in an arm chair with a stack of old newspapers on her lap. Most likely she's been clipping coupons.

You remember why your wife never liked coming here. The last time the three of you visited, the guest room reeked so intensely of cat urine that it was difficult to sleep. And then back home, days after the trip, the smell of the house lingered on your clothes, Owen's toys, even your bodies. No, Little Ma's colon cancer notwithstanding, you don't blame your wife for the six to one ratio of visits to her parents versus visits to yours.

Looking around the room, you realize you can make your peace with the cluttered house and the pack-rat mania; it's the refrigerators that you can't bear to open. There are three of them. One is in the kitchen and two are in the garage. One of the garage refrigerators is the old kitchen refrigerator that died but is "perfect for storing canned vegetables and dry goods" and the other was your grandmother's and is packed to the gills. In the olden days when you wanted, say, a glass of orange juice, you asked Mom if they had any, or you asked your wife to get it for you. She didn't mind and you knew she secretly enjoyed seeing what kinds of moldy fruits, green meats, soft cheeses gone hard, and funky condiments she'd find. One Christmas Eve she held out a bottle of something you couldn't identify and said, "I didn't think soy sauce could actually curdle." You've not looked in the refrigerator since she died.

You set down Owen on the kitchen floor. "Open the fridge, honey, and get the milk."

"Meeelk," he says.

"Yes, in the fridge. I'm in desperate need."

"Not dursty."

"I am."

"Cha-cha."

"Okay, you can have some. It's in the fridge, too."

As soon as he opens the door, you expect a load of condiments or overloaded plates or containers to come crashing down all around his feet. Broken glass, ketchup, pickles, and rancid food smells.

But nothing happens. Owen just stands there. "Cha-cha."

You peer in over his shoulder. The refrigerator is relatively clean. You step back to get a look, thinking that they might have bought a new one.

"Cha-cha."

"Sorry, looks like they're all out."

"Cha-cha!"

"Yes, yes, I know." You scoop him up and give him the tickle treatment. A classic move of distraction. Instead of giggling he's pulling at his ears again. Suddenly you see them. Fleas in his hair. "For chrissake's," you say aloud.

"Keees?"

"Christ," you say, but there's no time to explain. You take him back upstairs. "It's into the bathtub for you, mister."

After a good scrub and rechecking the bed for bugs, you get him to sleep without trouble. Now it's time: you find the yearbooks behind other books on the bottom shelf.

The first thing you do is look for a clue as to who sent you a mysterious email a couple of weeks ago: *How have you been? Hopefully shitty. See, its come to my attention that I never got to kick your ass. I know your coming to the reunion, so don't try to deny it. Never forget The Single Finger.* The note, signed *U R FUCT,* came from an email address you could only trace to somewhere in the Chicago area. Why did you ever bother to post your email address? For some reason you are more concerned with this person's inability to use the apostrophe than his (or her?) beating you up.

Although you never had many enemies in school or even now, you still scan the pages for any reference to "The Single Finger" in the handwriting of the people who signed your yearbook.

No luck. But you do find your entry in the "senior summaries." Goal: "To become a private investigator in Hawaii and to own a Ferrari." Jesus. Favorite teacher: "Mrs. Steffen." What? You remember hating her for making you write a paper on Matthew Arnold's "Dover Beach." What was the point, you told her, of reading this poem about the beach—if you want to experience the beach, wouldn't it be better simply to go to the beach? Your favorite memory: "Prom with LW and cross-country championship junior year." You glance over old classmates' summaries; under a name you recognize as a guy who ODed in college you read his goal: "To succeed."

You flip a few pages and find your senior photo. Major nerd. Does somebody want to smash your face for being a nerd? Then looking at the other headshots, you conclude that everyone is a nerd. The 80's was a decade of nerdism—even the cool kids were nerds. But today everyone, including the nerds, is cool. You turn the pages and quickly realize there are a lot of faces you don't want to ever see again. Dicks and bitches. Of the latter, though, you have to admit looking at some of their photos now does trigger the memory of innumerable masturbation sessions. There were those times, even after college, when you weren't dating anyone—you'd pull out the yearbook and imagine alternate lives with girls who you had crushes on in high school. It was beyond pathetic but it filled in the outline of loneliness.

You find the photos of the small clique of friends you had. At times a close group—advanced placement class takers but also dope-smokers and band members and cheerleaders. You remember an excerpt from Carmen's valedictorian speech word for word: *We should all be very proud of ourselves and our accomplishments given that it is hard to soar like eagles when we were led by a turkey.* The eagle was a reference to your school's mascot and the turkey was a reference to the principal. Carmen was probably the only student whose parents had to have a conference with the principal *after* their child graduated. But her parents didn't mind. In fact none of your parents would have minded. Since your class had been in elementary school, parents had talked about how special all of you were. They even differentiated you from siblings a year or two older or younger. You heard your mother once tell another mother on the phone, "He's going to do something spectacular in the sciences, don't ask me what, yes, I simply know it, biology, I think." You could picture the mother on the other end of the line nodding her head into the phone. Sadly, you did nothing in the sciences and the only biology you have is a tiny grasp of the workings of your colon because you were diagnosed with irritable bowel syndrome three years ago.

"Class of '88," your mother says, startling you, "you were special." You didn't even notice her come in—and since when is she a mind reader?

"*Were* special?" you say.

"Still are."

You suppose she is right, but not for the old reasons.

"Your sister's class was smart, but they didn't have the same ambition as yours."

"Do you remember when you tried to get me into gifted?"

"That program was a joke," she says. "You were gifted, you just didn't test well."

You debate about whether or not to tell her, and then you just say it, "I intentionally screwed up the test."

"What are you talking about? I had them give it to you twice."

"I screwed up the second one too."

"What?"

"I know you wanted me to be gifted, but I didn't want to be gifted."

"But you *were* gifted."

You note the past tense but don't say anything. Then you wonder if you want Owen to be gifted. Then another thought which you voice aloud: "What if Owen turns out to be retarded?"

She assures you that he's normal and bright and perfect.

"But will he test well?" you say.

She smiles now, thinking that you're kidding.

"Oh, look," she says, and points at a group photo of the pom-pom squad. "Isn't that Lane?"

"It's Julia."

"Really?"

"Lane was on the tennis team, Julia was in poms."

"I could never keep your harem straight."

"It wasn't a harem, Mom."

"Well, there certainly were a lot of girls."

"They were just friends, except for Lane."

"I didn't like her very much."

"I know," you say and then add, "in the end I didn't like her either."

"Carmen—she would have been a better first girlfriend for you."

This is probably true, except for the fact that you could never get yourself to be attracted to her.

"What's she doing now?"

You tell her you don't know and that, in fact, you've lost contact with everyone—Julia, Lane, Carmen, Rick—from your old clique.

"Did you ever go to your high school reunions?" you ask.

"I don't think they had any. You forget my high school was in a small farm town. Only twenty-five in my graduating class. Besides, I never would have had time to go back. We drove past the building once when we visited your grandmother years ago. Or I guess we drove past the spot where the building once was. Torn down, now a bank or something. It'll be interesting, though, for you to go tomorrow. There is one thing I'd like to know. Was it you or your sister who put the bullet hole in the Buick?"

"Elizabeth," you say. "She didn't put it there, I mean, the car apparently got hit one of those times she drove into the city with her friends to go clubbing."

"I figured as much," Mom says.

"You're not upset?"

"That was a long time ago, water under the bride and all."

You note her malapropism, a habit which over the years you've found more and more endearing. Your favorite is when she says *Variety is the price of life.*

"I'll leave you to it here," she says. "I've got laundry and stuff to do downstairs before your sister and George arrive tomorrow for brunch."

As soon as she leaves, you go digging into the desk for the photo of you and the harem—Julia, Lane, and Carmen. The Polaroid is a pseudo ménage à quatre—you are all fully clothed, wrapped up as in a game of Twister—but for some reason you don't want your mother ever to see it.

Before you even get into the second drawer, you find a small notebook and some scraps of paper with your father's handwriting. Some are dated within the last year.

You first found similar scraps of paper while you were home from college one summer. Rummaging around your bedroom, trying to find a t-shirt or sock or something, you came upon pages of legal pad paper that had been shoved, hastily it appeared, underneath a stack of books. The scribblings were so bizarre that some of the passages stuck in your mind verbatim, and then one day they seemed to vanish from your mind without you're noticing they'd vanished. But now, here are what look to be fairly new scribblings:

B put herself and others permanently in my head. Invasion of privacy is one huge issue. This is what I have to put up with.

Martha was a friend 7 times. Never married with her. No sex together. Martha was in Africa 7 times. And had to carry water 8 miles each morning. Had to live on the cusp of starvation. She had a son, same as now. She always tried to befriend those who came for help.

5 times I was on Atlantis.

Billy Bob Thorton - joined 12/9/06
Ozzie Osborn - joined
Mike Nichols - ?
Angelina Jolia
Unga = "boiling over"
Mr. Magic = me

Had 7 children, 3 stillborn (wife ate too much beef)

B had me clubbed to almost death 3 times this morning (12/13/06). And also whipped 80 lashes in my sleep. I was groggy again. But I broke B's noise with a mind bolt of energy.

I have been black 6 times.

Your stomach sinks and a pang of unidentifiable emotion runs the length of you. You'd assumed that he had stopped writing crazy notes. Your mother hasn't mentioned any others since those you showed her years ago. Your head pounds with thought in every direction. You sink to the floor in a daze.

You find her ironing in the basement. "Look at these," you say, handing her the papers.

"Yes," Mom says, "I've seen others like that."

"How many?"

"I don't know."

"Recently?"

"I don't know," she says, "I used to find them among the magazines in the copper tub near the fireplace. They were redundant so I stopped noticing them."

They may be redundant but they may also be sign of a psychological break. Or at least that's what you imagine, based mainly on nine months of reruns of crime scene TV shows; your attempt to beat insomnia. So while your mother continues to iron unperturbed, you go searching the house for more notes. An hour of Easter-egg hunting yields two small memo notebooks and an assortment of scribbled-on receipts, used envelopes, and post-it notes. You wonder if these coincide with the wine drinking.

When you display the evidence to your mother, she seems only a little concerned. "What about the voices?" you ask.

"I don't know," she says, cleaning the downstairs toilet. "Maybe he hears a few."

It's not the voices that trouble you exactly; it's what they might tell him. You remind her of the time he tried to transfer money from their savings account to some quasi-religious organization in Montana. The plan only failed because he got one of the digits in the bank's routing number wrong.

She acknowledges that the scraps could be a potential problem. You feel like you should do something.

"Whatever you do," she says, "don't take the papers with you. Put them back where you found them, so that he doesn't know we've seen them."

"Fine," you say, "but I'm making copies."

"If you want," she says, wrapping the toilet brush in a plastic bag.

"Do you have any change?"

"Check my purse."

It's difficult finding a copy machine in the middle of the night, but finally at a convenience store attached to a gas station you manage to copy, at a quarter per page, twenty or thirty pages of material. You pull the car back into your parents' driveway feeling better that you've done something. It's almost one a.m. and you're completely exhausted. At least you have the scribblings—you can analyze them later or take them to The Professor for his advice.

You open the front door and notice there's still a light on in the kitchen. Mom is sitting at the table with a cup of tea. You sit down more out of guilt for not having visited home in so long than out of any desire to talk.

"How's Owen taking it?"

You're surprised it took this long for her to ask, though you thought she'd ask how you were taking it. You'd like to tell her *fine* or *just dandy*. No, you'd really like to tell her that when one has a young child, one moves through Kübler-Ross a little differently than others: Denial is fairly easy and lasts about five minutes; Anger seems to be a continual stage that comes in unpredictable waves; Bargaining doesn't make any sense (how do you bargain with a dead woman?); and, Depression, though tempting, has to be skipped altogether, because if one doesn't get out of bed, it's not as if one's toddler is going feed himself breakfast, pack a well-balanced snack, and then navigate morning traffic to half-day daycare. As for Acceptance, the alleged final stage, one is still not sure what that might be; acceptance of what—the cliché that death is a natural part of life? It was only *too* natural that one's wife died because of a camouflaged tree nut. You want to tell your mother all of this. But it's too late and you don't have the energy for a drawn-out conversation. So after an extended meaningful pause, you say, "Honestly, Mom, I don't think it really matters. Owen's not even two, and soon enough he won't remember her at all."

"Certainly he'll remember his mother."

"What for?"

She stares at you blankly, or what you take to be blankly, and then the word itself *blankly* runs again and again through your head until finally she gets up from the table, turns off the kitchen light, and marches up the stairs to bed. You sit there for some time in the dark, with your head down on the table. As usual you contemplate suicide. As usual it seems like too much trouble.

3.

"Ma-ma! Ma-ma!"

You've woken up to these exclamation points before. Sometimes Owen does this in the morning: thinks his mommy is going to pick him up and smother him with kisses.

He screams again, with upraised arms.

"Who's my favorite boy!"

"Ma-ma, Ma-ma!"

You hold him—"Da-da, here, honey, Da-da"—tight enough to squeeze out his breath. "Quiches!" you say, imitating your wife's pronunciation of kisses. "Quiches!" and you kiss the boy's head until he sleepily giggles himself out of hysteria.

You look at your watch: 5:53. About the standard time. In the dark, you carry him downstairs. He enjoys making coffee with you because he likes the smell of the grounds.

An hour of playing with toys and an hour of walking around the neighborhood and you expect your mother to be up and about, but she's not.

Owen needs a change of scene and you want some air, so you decide to take your parents' car for a drive. As long as you're back for brunch around noon, nobody will care.

You head toward downtown. Twenty years ago, Algonquin wasn't much of a suburb, and even though it's grown from 3,000 to 30,000 inhabitants, it's still not much of one now. You recall what Mom used to say about Algonquin—that it's most renowned for once harboring Chicago's mafia, including Al Capone who had a summer bungalow along the Fox River that runs north-south through town; and that it's second most renowned for a long, sloping hill that runs parallel to the river, north up Route 31 to Crystal Lake. The mile-long hill at a 30 degree grade used to serve as a dramatic test run for cars in the 1920s. At least, that's what she always told you.

Owen is asleep by the time you pull onto Route 31, the main thoroughfare which is a clogged single-lane in each direction, a way to creep from one Chicago suburb to the next. Not far from the hill, Route 31 intersects Route 62 marking the center of Algonquin. You drive past the old town hall, which now looks empty, on the corner. When you were a kid, the town hall, which also housed the library and had a pool in the back, *was* the downtown, excepting a couple of divey pubs, a greasy spoon, a gas station, and a used car lot. There was one McDonald's in town, built when you were a sophomore, and the closest grocery store was ten miles away in the neighboring village of Dundee. You made that grocery run innumerable times, a seemingly long car ride without seatbelts, sitting in the back of the race-car red Duster, fighting with Elizabeth mostly out of boredom.

Elizabeth is such a pretty name. Whatever happened to the Elizabeth you knew as a kid, the one who read *David Copperfield* when she was six years old? Oh yes, she's still your younger sister, and she still lives in a suburb forty minutes south, Geneva. Suddenly you're aware of all the funny names of suburbs: Elgin (the forgotten clock and watch company), Palatine (something to do with the Romans?), Schaumburg ("mountain of foam," if your German is correct), Cicero, Harvard, Homer Glen, Sleepy Hollow, Libertyville, etc. Algonquin might be the best of them, in name, if nothing else. The Native Americans and the famous roundtable of writers and artists in New York City. And yet, you don't feel any special kinship to your hometown. It hasn't been your home for ages, and with three big box stores, seven supermarkets, and miles of subdivisions, it no longer resembles the place you once lived in. So be it. Change is the only constant, they say, and they are always right whoever they are. And besides you enjoy change. Never living in one place for more than two or three years, you've moved eight times (last time you bothered to count) since graduation. Elizabeth, on the other hand, has lived in Geneva for more than a decade, and although she's three years younger than you, she's been married for almost fifteen years to her college sweetheart, George.

If you are going to go through with this blast into the past tonight, you might as well scope out the venue: Harry D. Jacobs High. You take a left onto Route 62, hit Randall Road, and it'll be on the right about a mile down. Once in middle of a cornfield, it's now surrounded by wall-to-wall tract homes, large, well-meaning tract homes, actually. You see the sign in the distance. Underneath Harry D. Jacobs High School, Est. 1978, there's a stream of gold words on an LED sign…*Welcome Back Class of 1988!…Reunion Weekend!…September 12 & 13….*

As you approach you realize the long driveway to the school is no longer there. You slow down to where it used to be and park the car on the shoulder. Cars drive past doing sixty-five. You turn around and check on Owen in the backseat; he's snoring. Are you really going to do this? When you first heard of a possible twenty-year reunion, more than a year ago, you asked your wife what she thought. "You can go as long as I don't have to," she said, and then later when you brought it up again, "What— are you expecting to have the best moments of your life there?" You never answered her. You should have. You should have said that the best moments of your life were with her—especially that first year together and then right around Owen's first birthday, when you and she finally felt like real parents, real adults and couldn't get over how lucky you were to have such a sweet baby, and how you agreed wholly when one day she said, *Sometimes it scares me how much I love our boy, sometimes I feel like I'm going to explode.* The only other moments that come close to these are some great talks with The Professor in grad school in Memphis. Countless times you two pulled all-night drinking and writing sessions, feeding off each other's giddiness. Wishing you could hold onto those conversations, one night you tape-recorded the whole thing. The writing ceased around midnight, then there was some driving around midtown and Beale Street, grocery shopping at the Piggly Wiggly, drinking on the rooftop of your apartment building, going out in a desperate effort to seduce a couple of Russian undergrads (or were they high school girls?) at a dilapidated mansion-cum-bar called The Castle, and finally passing out on The Professor's front porch. You thought it'd be a terrible recording, a bunch of drunken nonsense, and most of it was, but there were some gems in there too—moments of "unbridled fucking genius" as The Professor calls them.

When you recently asked him about the reunion, he said, "Why not go, it'll be a kind of experiment."

"What kind?"

He mock-scratched his chin, a telltale sign that he was nearly drunk. "Social psychological—no—social anthropological."

"What?"

"Oh come on, it'll be like traveling in time but without the time machine. Think of the ramifications of examining your life narrative as compared to others' life narratives. A real biological confrontation. A fucking pivotal intertwining of your carefully constructed self identity vis-à-vis socially preponderant standards of success and accomplishment. Your situational identity and your personal identity will be at loggerheads."

"If you say so," you said and finished your beer. "By the way, wasn't your thirtieth a couple of years ago?

"Last year, actually."

"I don't remember you going."

"Of course not," said The Professor, "you think I wanted to subject myself to some asshole's, no, some group of assholes's Durkheimian-cum-Peter-Panian trip down memory lame."

"I'd have thought you'd want the experience for research material?"

"Anecdotal at best, and I have enough from my tenth and twentieth. At the tenth, people had barely gotten their personal identities established—a lot of poorly veiled one-upmanship. The women who were hot in high school were still hot and the men who were fated to go bald were already bald. Frankly the men were uniformly boring and mostly wanted to get their pee-pees wet. Anyway, by the twentieth, people were well ensconced in their situational identities—"

"Their what?"

"Their lives, friend. *Lives*. I'll admit there were anthropological issues concerning community and a great deal of souls in need of community and trying, ever so slightly, to get some by mining their high school days for a community that never really existed. All this, mind you, around a table of raw vegetables, ranch dip, and Danish butter cookies. Fucking light beer. Everyone expressed happy indifference toward each other. If they were truly happy with their lives, their spouses, the kids, then they were happy and didn't need to talk to you to compare notes. If they were unhappy, then they'd learned to accept their situational personality, knowing that it was too late to get out. In the end the best piece of data I sequestered had to do with interpersonality and alcohol. As in high school, when a couple of friends would sneak a beer or two before class, folks acted drunker than they were. Like drinking was still the epitome of cool."

"All right already," you said, "I won't go."

"No, I think you should go. I want you to verify my experience."

Experience, you think, is not something you want more of at the moment. You'd prefer a nap. No sooner do you close your eyes and begin to fade away, when you hear mild squawking from the backseat. You don't mean to, but sometimes you forget Owen is there. It's probably the occasional bursts of noise from the semitrucks and the lack of movement that are beginning to wake him. His eyes are still closed, but his little lips are smacking together slowly. If you get moving again, he'll stay asleep. You give Harry D. Jacobs the middle finger and pull back onto the road.

There's still an hour and a half to kill before brunch. You head south on Randall Road, noticing the newest stores to go up in the cornfields you used to run along in cross-country practice, and soon your thoughts turn again to Alex Mueller. He was your closest friend and rival on the cross-country team. The moment that sticks out most is when he told you about how his grandfather and a few other teenagers in Auschwitz chipped in to get a prostitute so they wouldn't have to die virgins. "So what do you say?" Alex asked you and a teammate, "it'll only cost fifty bucks each." You declined, hoping you wouldn't have to die before actual sex would take place with Lane.

You heard from a friend of a friend that Alex is going to be in Chicago on business and plans to attend the reunion. You told this to The Professor last time you saw him at the gym.

"Are you gay?" he said, loading the bench press for you.

"What do you think?"

"I wouldn't be asking if I didn't have suspicions."

The weights felt heavier than usual. Weightlifting was one of the first of The Professor's suggestions. He kept saying that the tension would find a detrimental outlet if you didn't give it a healthy outlet.

"He's just an old track buddy," you said, putting down the bar. "I don't know what the fixation is. He was a friend, not a best friend. I just have this intuitive feeling he's done something interesting, something—"

"You're not going to say *profound*, are you?"

"Take off some of this weight. Are you trying to kill me?"

"Let me do a set, then I'll change it."

In between breaths, The Professor stammered out, "This… latent…homo…sexuality…When do…you think…it began?"

"It's not homosexuality. I'm just curious."

He sat up and wiped his forehead. "A serious disparity lies between who or what you think you are and what or who you think other people think you are. It's a matter of performance. To put it in layman's terms, it's like you're the director, the actor, and the audience of a play. And that play is being filmed from backstage by a voyeur."

You had no idea what he was talking about, as usual, but it did strike you as vaguely poetic.

"Voyeur?" you said, "do you mean I'm starring in my own porn?"

After another set, he said, "I hadn't thought about it like that, but sure. Okay, yes, in that milieu, I suppose we could say you're trying to have intercourse with yourself via Alex Mueller. Boomerang autophilia is the proper term."

Before you know it you're halfway to your sister's house. In an effort to turn around and after a U-turn that nearly clips another car, you get confused and end up on I-90 West. You consider "West" for a moment—the Heroes and Anti-Heroes course you taught last spring, how Huck Finn lit out for the West; you consider not going back to your parents' house, driving out to your dead grandmother's hometown in Iowa, four hours away; you consider not stopping there either and continuing to Colorado, hell, all the way to California, visit some old college friends in San Francisco. But you know you can't do any of this; you don't really like San Francisco anymore and Owen is going to be hungry when he wakes up and pulling over to feed him would interrupt your momentum and you'd never make it farther than the Mississippi.

Coming up Randall Road again you see someone with a backpack walking on the side of the road. It looks an awful lot like Alex. Mirage?

Suddenly an enthusiastic *Daa-daa!* rings out from the backseat.

You can't slow down to get a better look anyway, not in this traffic.

"It's okay, hon, we'll be at grandma and grandpa's soon. Have to stop at the grocery store first. Grandma needs butter and eggs." Not true, but running around the aisles will keep the little guy occupied. You're still ten minutes away from the store, though, and Owen is definitely awake and grumbling. To keep him happy in situations like this, where you can't play or read a book with him face-to-face, you often engage him in conversation about whatever is on your mind.

"Tell me again," you say, hitting the gas, "how much do you think about Mommy? No, I won't take notes this time, and you're not obliged to stick to your answer in subsequent interrogations. Yes, I know you didn't know her for very long, but she was a beauty and a mensch and she loved you like the dickens."

You adjust the rearview mirror so that you can see his face

better. He's staring at you, sucking his thumb, which is not a habit except when he wants to feel especially comforted.

"How often do I think about her, you ask? Well, the answer to that would take more time perhaps than we have before our arrival at the store. In any case, I knew Mommy very well— you'll have to take my word for it—and...oh...I see...an afterlife? I don't know if there is one—I mean, maybe you can tell me since you were there recently—is there a beforelife?"

Owen makes his noise for what a bird sounds like.

"I guess it is a strange question, but you see my point. Even if there is a beforelife or afterlife, without who you are now, without that beautiful little body of yours, my sweet prince, it won't matter. What matters then? My best answer—and I don't mean to be glib as I know you take things to heart, and perhaps you are a bit too sensitive at times, if I may say so—but my best answer is that she still lives inside of you. Yes, that's right, in your DNA. What—how does she live inside of me then? I know I don't have any of her DNA, except as you well know the strands of her hair which I keep finding in odd places around the house and storing in a plastic baggie in my sock drawer. I know, I know, it's foolish if not cliché. But she lives, to answer your question, in my mind."

You check the rearview. He's looking out the window in a daze at the subdivisions racing by.

"It's not the answer you wanted, I can tell. It's all right if you want to be mad at me. I can take it. I am really tough that way. Besides I realize your ears must be tired. I know from years of experience that your grandma can talk an ear off. On those once-a-month, two-hour phone calls, I get cauliflower ear—in both ears! Yes, my mother, not Little Ma. Did I ever tell you the story of my mother making me pay for long-distance? Before cell phones when I would visit your grandma, say, around a holiday, I would occasionally make phone calls to whatever girlfriend I had at the time. A month later your grandma would send me a photocopy of her phone bill with my calls highlighted. She would then expect a check for $12.56 or whatever it was. I suppose I should have predicted this, as it came from the same woman who avoided the unlisted phone number fee by using her maiden name in the phone book."

He looks back at you in the mirror with a funny face.

"I am sorry I raised my voice."

He continues the face.

"Really, you sympathize with her?"

He continues the face and now gives you his intense eyes look.

"What is it, my lad? Oh that, under my lower lip? That is a nice scar, isn't it. I never think about it or notice it until someone else does. Shape of a cosign wave, you're right. I think, it could be a sine wave—I don't remember much math. I got that when I was about your age. Your grandpa was carrying me down the stairs—and oops!—he tripped and out I tumbled. No, I don't remember it. But that is at least the story they tell me. Of course I believe the story, I'm not trying to insinuate abuse, far from it. If anything, I think your grandma and grandpa loved me too much as a kid. Me? Yes, I love you too much too. But I assure you I am extra-careful on the stairs. Your grandma wouldn't let your grandpa carry me after that little incident for a couple of years, which, yes, now that you mention it, may have influenced my relationship with him subsequently."

Wheeling around the parking lot in a cloudburst of rain, you finish your discourse just in time to find a spot near to the front door of the grocery store. You lift Owen out of his seat and shuttle him inside. It's impossible to tell which one of you is more relieved to be out of the car.

4.

There he is again taking photos. Your father loves the camera and you have to admit that over the years he's gotten some good candid shots. You show him your digital camera. He's never used one before, so he takes it to the kitchen table, and says he's going to figure out how it works. You and Elizabeth bring the little ones into the family room. You sit on the carpet since the armchairs and sofa are piled with newspapers and magazines.

Pearl is showing Owen how to flip pancakes in the play kitchen set, sitting on the fireplace's hearth. You eye the copper tub. What if Owen has a copper allergy? You've been meaning to get a whole work up of skin tests for him.

After a couple of minutes your sister says, "Owen looks happy."

"He is."

"His hair," she says, "it's so much lighter than yours."

"Lighter than his mother's was too," you add.

There's a predictable silence.

"Did Mom yell at Dad all morning?"

You could tell her that you think Dad is doing even less housework than usual. You and your sister are used to Mom's nagging him, and though you would never tell Elizabeth this, she and George have a similar pattern of arguing.

"I don't know," you say, "I ran some errands."

"You left Owen here?"

"No, he came with me."

"You can leave him here, you know. Mom and Dad baby-sit for us once a month. Mom made homemade play-dough last time. Pearl loved it."

"I remember eating that stuff," you say, "extra salty."

"Like the cat food you ate."

Pearl has moved on to flipping plastic hamburger patties, making Owen lunch.

"I only ate the hard stuff," you say, "never that wet mush, and I remember especially liking the chicken and egg triangles."

"That's *disgusting*," Elizabeth says in a tone like Mom used to use. You both laugh.

No longer interested in Pearl's cooking show, Owen is playing with a couple of Fisher-Price people, who appear to be mostly bald from a lot of use.

"How do you think Dad's doing?"

"Same, I guess."

"I didn't want to tell you this," you say, "but I found some of his scribblings again."

"Scribblings?"

From your pocket you pull out a couple of the photocopies. She looks at them and doesn't seem surprised. Maybe she found some herself years ago. One of those hundreds of afternoons she spent sitting, after school, watching TV with him, neither of them saying a word. You still feel guilt for going off to college, but you also know escaping this house saved you. Finally she says, "These look pretty innocuous."

"Really?"

"I've seen worse."

As a social worker she probably has.

"The stuff about using coconut and olive oil to prevent wrinkles," she says, "that's kind of funny. And this thing about meat causing fifty-seven different diseases—hell, that's probably true."

"What about these," you say, pulling out another page.

When Martha is home she cannot bother me with projects or I will have to get an apartment. We cannot live together without malice so we have to get a legal separation by the law of Illinois. No one can fool around. This is so that no one can claim abandonment.

"Well," she says, "that explains Dad's not fixing that hole in the ceiling from the bathtub leak."

"Are they getting a divorce?"

"They probably should have years ago, but I don't think so now," she says, and points, "look at the date, this entry is three years old."

"What about this other one. He talks about being a hover craft pilot on Atlantis in 5000 BC," you say.

But before you can find the entry, she says, "As long as he doesn't call the FBI again, it'll be fine. He lives in his own head. Besides the endless grocery shopping that drives mom nuts, he probably functions as well as the rest of us. Sometimes I think it'd be better if Mom just let him alone. What is he—seventy-two this year? Let him enjoy what's left. And I'll tell you one more thing—I think Mom didn't do him any favors going to her psychics all those years, asking for predictions about you and me and especially his illness."

"It fed his delusions?"

"Probably. I bet she still sees a psychic. Before Pearl was born, Mom told me things the psychic said about the baby."

"I know we don't talk about it much," you say, "but I think

we're lucky to be adopted. It really hit me after Owen was born."

"Do you remember," she says, "when Mom showed us how to check our wrists to see if we could have kids?" She takes your hand, turns it over, and traces the line between your palm and wrist. "See, an unbroken line means you can have kids—broken, like Mom's, means no kids."

"Why couldn't she have kids?"

"I don't know, but I remember she never got her period, and when I did, she didn't really know what to do."

"You ever check Pearl's wrist?"

"You're talking about me?" Pearl says.

You and your sister both assure Pearl it is nothing.

"What were you saying!" she says.

"Only good things," you say, "like how sweet you are with your cousin Owen."

"Pearl, where's Owen?"

After a desperate if brief hunt, you find him in the bathroom.

"Do you have to go pee-pee?"

He shakes his head.

"Well, Daddy has to go."

As you unzip, Owen pulls the toilet paper off into a small pile. Then he flushes for you; three times just to make sure.

"No hands in the toilet bowl," you say, as he tries subtly to make the move.

You lift him up and wash his and your hands. You notice his nose is running and the mucus is a light green. Lovely another ear infection. Most likely the plane ride. Another reason never to fly again.

When you return to the family room, Dad is sitting in his recliner. At first you think he's crying and you rush over, "What is it?"

Then you see he's laughing so hard there are tears in his eyes. Elizabeth points to the camera he's holding. It's a photo of Owen you took last night in the bathtub. Pearl wants to see. George and your mother come in from the kitchen. Everyone thinks Owen looks very handsome in his shampoo Mohawk, sporting one of his stellar smiles.

Your mother's brunch looks like Thanksgiving dinner. Glazed ham, mashed potatoes, roasted eggplant, three-bean salad, cucumber salad, honeyed carrots, garlic bread, a tray of assorted pickles, olives, and beets, mixed berry punch (Pearl's favorite), and, for dessert, cobbler with blueberries straight from the backyard. It is truly a lovely dining room table.

After Dad says grace, everyone digs in. There's a lot of healthy commotion and passing of dishes. You mound your plate with some of everything, but then can't seem to do much with it. Everyone else goes at it like a glutton. You focus on Owen getting enough to eat.

Your mother shows the kids how to put black olives on their fingers. "As a little boy," she says to Owen, "your daddy would only eat olives this way. He said they tasted like licorice."

Pearl winces.

"You like licorice," George says to her.

"I don't like olives," she says.

"What kind of Greek girl doesn't like her olives?"

George believes all the best things in the world have come from Greece where his parents were born. He's always going on about the importance of family and food. Which shows—he must be up over 300 pounds now.

"Feta is really good," you say.

"Damn right, and retsina, too," he says and lifts his wine glass, "Dad, you have any more of this vino?"

Without your asking, Dad tops off your glass too.

"I don't care for the stuff."

"Everyone knows you don't drink, Mom," Elizabeth says.

"I meant feta, it's just plain gross," Mom says and sours up her face.

"I'll eat those olives," Elizabeth says to Pearl. "George will you throw them on my plate?"

"No," he says. "Pearl, down the gullet with those olives."

George and Elizabeth begin arguing about whether or not she has to eat them.

"Let's let Dad settle it," you say. "What are the antioxidant properties of olives?"

But Dad is at an angle where his bad ear is facing you.

"Dad?"

"Oh, he doesn't fucking know," George says.

"I didn't ask you, asshole."

"That's enough," Mom says. "Time for dessert."

She goes into the kitchen and comes back with the blueberry cobbler and fresh whipped cream.

"Blueberries are very high in antioxidants."

"We know, Dad," George says.

"Wine, too. Red not white. And kale, Russian kale. We have some in the garden. Martha, where was the kale?"

"I hear goji berries have the most antioxidants of all," Elizabeth says.

"Never heard of them," Dad says. "But pomegranates are high too. Do you want some pomegranate juice? I have a bottle in the fridge."

"No one wants any pomegranate juice," Mom says.

Owen hears the word "juice" and goes wild. Your mom gets some juice from the kitchen.

"How's work, George?" Dad says.

"Same as always. Too much management. My boss wants me to go to D.C. for a convention."

"The sea?" Dad says.

"D.C.—Washington."

"Those guys are all crooks," Dad says. "They covered up JFK."

"Dad," you say, "we saw the movie."

"The movie got most of it right," he says, "but it didn't go into what Congress did. The whole lot of them were in on it."

At least once every time you visit, Dad manages to work JFK into the conversation. Usually you let it go.

"All of Congress?" you say.

"Yes, you don't believe me?"

"I don't know. Not everything's a conspiracy."

"Damn near," Mom offers.

"I bet someone poisoned your wife with that cashew," Dad says.

For a moment the room is completely silent. Everyone—even Owen and Pearl—is looking at you. Or it feels that way; you're looking down at the plate.

"I decided to go to the reunion tonight."

"Good," Mom says.

"Yes, that's wonderful," Elizabeth says.

"Probably won't stay for the whole thing. But it starts before Owen's bedtime. Mom, could you put Owen to bed?"

"I can stay," Elizabeth says, "to help."

"How are you going to do that?" George asks.

"We'll stay until Owen is asleep."

Before the argument gets going, Mom says she'll be happy to do it. "It'll give me a chance to spend time with my grandson."

After dessert, you volunteer to do the dishes if someone will look after Owen. Your parents don't believe in the dishwasher, so it'll take a while. You're counting on that. Then Mom offers to wash, remembering how you prefer to dry.

You haven't dried the first dish, when she says, "I don't think it was on purpose."

"Poisoning?"

"Your father saying it out loud just now. He brought it up the first time a couple of months ago when Elizabeth and George were over for dinner. We heard him out, but no one actually believed his theory."

"Theory? I've heard enough."

"He thinks she was poisoned by one of your students."

"For god's sake. Why are you telling me this?"

You toss down the towel and go in search of Owen. You flare—not because you think Dad is right or even that he has conjured up this harebrained idea, but because Mom wouldn't share your concerns last night. Don't fantastical scribblings merit the same worth as murder theories?

You find him in the living room, playing with grandpa. There's nothing to do but ignore the last thirty minutes of your life.

You lure Owen into the car seat with chocolate, and then he, your mother, sister and niece take off to do some shopping. That leaves you, Dad, and brother-in-law. It's beautiful weather out so you suggest throwing the football around. Even if Dad has never been much of a communicator, he has always been receptive to playing sports with you. Countless evenings when you were a boy, you dragged him outside at dusk to play catch.

You convince George to come out too. But you know he is dying to talk to you about Dad or your wife or a combination of the two. Somehow he thinks all the drama is fun. You find a spot on the front lawn far enough away from him so that he can't ask anything too intimate.

Dad's spirals are as good as ever but he still won't throw the football over your head, as you want him to, for the challenge of making the grab. Despite being athletic when he was younger (at least that's the story he's always put forth), George can't throw the ball for shit. He's the first to want to head back in. It's been fifteen minutes. You want to keep throwing in silence. You could do this all afternoon in silence. You wish you didn't have to speak, not just with members of your family, but later at the reunion. What if you played deaf tonight? It'd never work without practice. Why didn't you practice? Enjoy this quiet, wordless time now, outside, throwing the football mindlessly back and forth, trying to get each spiral tighter.

George goes into the house.

"A few more, Dad?"

He acquiesces, and the tosses continue. Your mind reels back to Saturday mornings last year. The happy little family in Audubon Park. Usually you played touch football with a bunch of lawyers while your wife and son strolled the walking path or played on a blanket. You still play football on Saturdays and someone's girlfriend or wife is always eager to look after your son. They all know where your wife is but no one talks about it. Playing isn't really the same, of course, since she's not there to watch you catch a game-winning bomb in the end zone or make a game-winning interception. It's amazing—she always seemed to get back to the field just in time for your best plays and would describe them back to you on the walk home.

When Dad's arm gets tired, you say you'd like to go around back and look at the vegetable garden. They have always had a garden that takes up a full third of the backyard, and you've always liked poking about, picking cherry tomatoes, admiring baseball bat-sized zucchini, and pushing away thick blue-green leaves to reveal heads of broccoli. You're looking at an eggplant trying to determine if it's ready to be picked when Dad beckons you to a patch of squash and pumpkins.

"Those look great," you say and bend down to give one of the pumpkins a knock.

"It's because of the elementals," he says and turns over the pumpkin. "Not ready yet."

"Elementals?"

"People give them different names around the world. In Ireland, they call them leprechauns. I'm sure you've heard about those."

From experience you know he's not kidding, but it's difficult not to smile. You ask him what the elementals do exactly.

"They keep the energy positive in the earth, cultivate the soil, if you will. The elementals in charge of the earth are actually called gnomes."

He tells you this as if you've never heard of a gnome, but you also didn't know gnomes were assigned to vegetable gardens. The two of you move to the compost pile where he begins turning the mulch over with a shovel. You lend a hand with a hoe.

"The British beat back the Norsemen because they," he says, "the British, I mean, ate red meat and built up bigger muscles. The Norsemen only had fish, so they were weaker."

You think this over and then try to point out that perhaps the Norsemen were simply outnumbered or outgunned or out-speared or whatever it was they killed each other with.

But Dad won't have anything of it.

A few more turns of the shovel and the mulch is well mixed. You both decide it's time to go back inside.

Dad says he's going to go meditate and heads for the family room. In your family lingo, meditating is best described as napping upright in a recliner, mouth propped open as if with a toothpick. George is fixing something in the kitchen, banging things around. You sense brother-in-law is in a bad mood. Maybe you caused it.

"Want to watch the game?"

"Which one?"

"Michigan and Notre Dame."

"I'd rather watch the Cubs. They're still in the hunt, only four back."

You should have predicted this. Brother-in-law's fixation on the Cubs. He has an entire room full of pennants, jackets, signed baseballs, and other memorabilia. This obsession is so serious that your sister and he aren't going to have another child because he'd have to give up his special room.

He finishes making a ham sandwich and offers you half.

"No thanks," you say, though you maybe should have said yes, as a way of making nice.

"Come on," he says, "let's watch the football game."

Dad is already asleep in front of the TV. He won't notice if you change the channel, though you have to keep the volume high, as he likes it, or he'll wake up.

The game is tied 7-7 in the first quarter. George likes Michigan to win and you agree. You wonder if talking like this with your brother-in-law is a cliché of masculinity. You don't care. You love college football. Your wife made you love it. You hadn't watched any in years, but then a couple of falls ago she began watching it. She couldn't come up with a reason for her new love except that she felt she was pregnant with a boy, and when you went for the sonogram, sure enough there was a penis suspended between two thighs. This cemented all subsequent Saturday afternoons: you and your wife and a bowl of popcorn watching one college game after another. It didn't matter who was playing, you watched them all, even if the picture was terrible on your ten-year-old TV set. She picked her favorite teams based on star players or team colors. City or state didn't seem too important, and mostly you agreed with her. Midwestern teams usually had advantage over West Coast teams and Southern teams. You reminded her that most East Coast teams were uniformly awful, especially the Ivy Leagues. So in the bowl games you picked Michigan over USC, Ohio State over Texas, and Penn State over Florida. Both of you heartily rooted for underdogs, like Boise State and Oregon.

On a commercial break George switches over to the Cubs' game. They are playing the Giants and are behind, 7-2. You watch a few pitches.

"The break is probably over—flip it back."

He changes it back just in time for you to see the ball sailing down the sideline. Notre Dame interception.

"Shit."

"What's your problem?" he says.

What's your problem? Is he a total fucking idiot?

"I don't have one. Do you?"

Another commercial. He flips back to the Cubs. Dad snorts, opens his eyes for a second, and then is back asleep.

You get up to use the bathroom. Afterward, instead of going back to the family room, you climb the stairs to your old bedroom. You lie down on the bed and use Owen's stuffed tiger for a pillow. One more look at the yearbook. There's something folded over and tucked inside a back page. Was this here before? You open the piece of notebook paper. It's a list of "Hates" and "Likes," dated October 30, 1985, your sophomore year. Under "Hates" is *school, teachers, freshmen, seniors, juniors, sister, weekdays, and waking-up.* Jesus Christ, you think, was I that miserable? Under "Likes" is *sports, pizza, french fries, swimming, soccer, Hawaii, cooking, sleeping, and summer.* Were you this bor-ing? You read further and can't quite figure out who wrote this. Woody Allen is in the wrong column—you love Woody Allen! Suddenly you have a terrible thought—will you be this differ-ent twenty-some-odd years into the future? At least one thing resonates: you like to sleep. Or rather you *would* like to sleep. Since she died your sleep is fitful, no matter how long you stay in bed. And you no longer dream. Or you don't remember dream-ing. You used to go through two- and three-week stints of vivid dreaming every night. It doesn't make sense; your brain should be doing overtime catharsis. A nightmare would be preferable to nothing. Then you disagree with this thought and go back and forth unable to figure out if you would rather experience terrible nightmares every night (maybe you could get used to them and they would become innocuous) or have absolutely no dreams for the rest of your life.

You wake to the sound of the front door slamming and children yelling and shrieking. You head downstairs. Owen is chasing Pearl up and down the hallway.

"Did Owen sleep in the car?" you ask your sister.

"He dozed the last ten minutes."

Now Pearl is chasing Owen. You worry that he's going to trip and smash his face. What if he cuts himself and gets one of those scars that doesn't go away—what are they called, keloids? You are about to pick him up when your sister puts an arm around you. "You okay?"

"I'm fine."

You can't handle it any longer and pick up Owen.

"What's fine?" she says.

"Somewhere between coarse and microscopic."

"Good one." She smiles. If anything, you've always been

able to make your sister laugh on demand, usually by doing your Chauncey voice. Chauncey was a character you made up as a kid, someone to blame things on when Mom wanted to know who started the fight, who broke this or that household object, etc.

Your niece tugs at your pant leg. She wants to be held too. With a child in each arm, you walk into the family room to play. Dad is still asleep in front of the blaring TV.

"Turn that thing down," says Mom from the kitchen.

"You've got to get Dad a hearing aid," Elizabeth says.

"I've tried. He won't use one."

"Try harder."

You spy *The Little Engine That Could* on the floor near the sofa and read it to the kids. You want to make this moment extra-special for them, so you invoke Chauncey's nasally voice.

"You're funny," Pearl says.

"Thank you," you say, and continue reading.

The book is one of your favorites from childhood, though you've never read it to Owen. The images of the smiling oranges and apples and the toy giraffes and elephants peeking out of the train window are vivid, if not on the page, then in your memory. You're surprised to find that the blue train is the one that reaches the top of the mountain; you have always thought it was the yellow one. For some reason you find this distressing. When you turn the last page, you expect more than the train engine merely making it to the top of the mountain. Somehow the story seems incomplete.

"Again," Pearl says, "again!"

"I'm sorry, lovey, that's all the lame narrative I can handle today."

"What's *lame*?"

"When a soldier gets his leg injured and it never heals properly and then he limps."

She just looks at you.

You decide you'd better read the book again.

Mom sets out leftovers on the kitchen counter. Everyone makes a plate. It's a tight squeeze around the kitchen table. You try to feed Owen but he's at the stage where he wants to do everything himself. You're used to the mess. You look around. You're used to this house, too, these people—sometimes you think of them as that—these people. They could be anyone. You could be anyone. But nobody isn't anybody. Your head is a sloppy mess. You equivocate about going tonight. Maybe you should hole up at one of the fake Irish pubs out by the strip malls.

Dad pours you a glass of wine. You immediately take it halfway down.

You keep weighing the pros and cons. A change of scene would be nice, until you remember that the reunion is at the high school. What is wrong with your head?

These people are talking about what kind of potatoes make the best mashed potatoes. Mom has a definite opinion—yellow potatoes—but brother-in-law is advocating a mix of red and fingerling. Potatoes?

Suddenly Owen coughs and then makes a terrible face. He's choking. "Are you okay?" You launch up from the table in a panic. "Are you okay!" Just as you're about to give him a hard back blow, his cough clears and he spits up on the table.

No one is disconcerted. Mom says: "Down the wrong pipe, little fella?"

You explode. "He could have chocked to death! Who gave him that grape! They're not even cut in half properly. You can't half-ass the grape cutting."

"It was a piece of pickle," Elizabeth says.

"What do you mean it was a piece of pickle?"

"It was a piece of pickle!"

"Chill out," George says, "both of you."

You detest that phrase, but you sit back down. Owen seems a little shocked by the outburst. You give him a carefully peeled grape cut into quarters, and he gives you a smile.

Mom starts talking about one of your second cousins, Donny or Davey or Dinky, and how he had ten teeth at ten months and could eat grapes whole. You want to say that's ridiculous but you don't like to argue with her. You remember teaching Jonathan Swift for the first time last year and one particular line comes to mind: *You can't argue somebody out of a position they never argued themselves into.* Or something like that, you've never been very good with direct quotes. She is talking about another cousin now and a distant relative who raises sand hill cranes in Nebraska. It's hard for you to keep up, even though she works in these updates regularly during your once-a-month phone conversations. You've tried to take an interest in extended family matters—Dad having nine brothers and sisters—but it's always a lost cause. You don't live near any of them and it doesn't make sense to stay in touch. Relatives may care about your parents, but what do they care about some high school teacher who lives five states away? You think of how much your wife didn't enjoy Mom's monologues. Mom always told you she wanted a close relationship with your wife, but she couldn't figure out how. Your wife never told you outright, but she really didn't like your mom. One grew up on a farm in Iowa in the fifties and the other grew up in New York City in the eighties. Why fault either of them?

Owen is playing with his food now—smashing pickled beets into the table and nonchalantly dropping peas, one by one, over the side. He didn't eat very much again. Another sign of depression?

Maybe it's you who's depressed. You expected The Professor to suggest it, but Little Ma beat him to it. "Get him to take some Prozac," you overheard her tell your sister-in-law at the funeral service. Sister-in-law disagreed: "Zoloft is better, if not trendier." Thank god you don't live close to them. One thousand miles from the in-laws and one thousand miles from your parents. That was the unspoken agreement between you and your wife. In any case, you never wanted to pop pills. You would go through this au naturel like your wife did giving birth. Little Ma may have been screaming *Get the epidural!* in the background, but your wife refused it. You couldn't afford a midwife or doula, so you played amateur coach: *You're almost over this contraction, you're at the top of it, almost, almost…you can do it….* You know your wife would want you to follow her lead.

With the serving spoon Mom finishes the pasta salad from the bowl. You know this disgusts your sister, but you've stopped caring. Does this make you better or worse than your sister?

"Can I bathe him later?" Mom says, wiping beet juice from Owen's face.

"He had one last night, but sure." You lift him out of the high chair. "Just remember to fill the tub only an inch or two."

Apparently Elizabeth, George, and Pearl are going to stay a while longer. Dad goes out to get a few movies from the public library. "Best selection in town," he says, "and you can't beat the price."

Everyone else heads to the living room since it's the least cluttered space in the house. Elizabeth asks if Mom can get out the old photo albums to show Pearl and Owen what you and she looked like as kids.

Before Mom can move the boxes and books blocking the

china cabinet, George says to her, "How about that Super 8 movie—what was that nineteen seventy-one, two? You sure were hot."

"What are you talking about?" she says.

Oh shit.

He starts to explain how you sent him a digital video of a Super 8 from when you were a one-year-old.

"I never saw that," she says, looking at you. "How did you get that?"

"I borrowed—"

"You took it from me! Where is it now? You know I don't like it when you steal—"

"I wasn't stealing. I found all those Super 8's—there must be thirty of them—in a box. They're still sealed, no one's ever seen them."

"It's stealing and I don't think much of it. Where is the one you took?"

You try to explain how you only wanted to see if Owen looks like you did as a toddler. (You leave out the part about his being your only blood-relative.) You tell her you know she'd never have the video transfer done—it's ridiculously expensive. But your friend The Professor has a Super 8 movie projector, and it was easy to capture it with your digital camera from the projected image. Mom doesn't care, however, about watching the actual footage—she only wants to know where the Super 8 film is.

"It's at home," you say, "I'll mail it as soon as I get back."

"You certainly will," she says, and stomps out of the room.

"I didn't know—" George starts.

"It's fine," you say. Though you suspect he knew what he was doing.

"Mom does look hot in it," Elizabeth says.

"What's *hot*?" Pearl asks.

"It's like when a soldier comes home from the war," you say, "and he sees a woman in a dress for the first time in months and—"

"Jesus," George says, and reaches over to cover her ears but misses, "what's with you?"

You thought you were lightening the mood.

"It's when someone looks pretty," your sister says. "Very pretty."

"That's Dad's car driving up," you say. You pick up Owen and carry him outside. No one is there. You wait on the front porch anyway, passing the time by letting Owen pull greenery off the shrubs. When Dad arrives, he has a small stack of movies: *Bowling for Columbine, The Matrix, X-Files,* and *From Russia With Love.* Though a good James Bond flick is usually appealing, this solidifies your decision.

After a quick shower and a small dilemma as to what to wear, you settle on dark blue jeans, a white button-up, and a corduroy jacket. An extra polish of deodorant under the arms and a cursory brush of the teeth. You're ready to go. The family, minus Mom, gives you the send off at the door. You tell Owen to be a good boy and kiss and hug him goodnight. When you hand him over to your sister, he screams and grabs for you as if he's drowning. You are tempted to stay, just so he doesn't have to drown like that. You stand there staring at him, until finally your sister says: "You're making it worse—*just go!*"

5.

You slowly coast by the building. Except for the entrance trimmed in gold and brown balloons (school colors), it looks like nothing has changed at all. Typical 1970s minimalist architecture. The fifteen-foot tall windows that line the front of the building are permanently yellowed by a combination of the sun's rays and a plexiglass maker's mistake. The only distinguishing feature of the building is the four-story arch at the front entrance, which looks like a miniature version of the St. Louis Arch. Strange how you never noticed that until now.

Behind the arch on the third floor there used to be the science laboratory, where Mr. Haraburda turned you on to biology freshman year and then turned you away from it by senior year. Though it was probably your own teenage fickleness, marine biology still sounds like a fun occupation were it not for your fear of deep water.

You pull into the parking lot where there are about ten cars. You'd better park out by the tennis courts, around the side of the building; you don't want anyone to think your parents' beater is actually yours. When you turn the corner, you see that ten more cars—only one of them looks like a beater—are already parked there.

On the way into the building you pass by a small group of

men in the parking lot. They're listening to football on a car radio. "Who the hell scheduled this thing during the game?" one of them says. You wonder if Michigan is doing any better against Notre Dame. For a second, you think you recognize one of the men as an old classmate who once conned the chemistry teacher into making something approximating napalm. But after a double-check you are fairly sure it's not the same guy and decide to pass by the men with a head nod.

The first thing you have to do is find Julia. Julia Baumholder, your best female friend in high school, and Jackie Shimko, voted most likely to organize a twenty-year high school reunion, have been planning this evening since last spring. They even managed to convince the principal to have the reunion at the high school—which hasn't apparently happened in more than a decade.

Julia was the lead actress in all the school plays. Junior year she's the one who got you to come out of your shell. It's hard to remember how she did it exactly, but it was likely the example she set—wearing hippy clothes and sporting peace necklaces at a time when preppy and polo was the order of the day, saying what she felt and not playing the usual cliquey games of high school. She taught you not to care what other people thought about how you looked or what you did. She taught you something simple and yet profound: to go on your nerve, a lesson you still carry around.

For the first years of college you two kept in touch. Halloween of sophomore year you took a bus up to Madison. She already had changed her major to communications and was living with her future husband, Thad, who she'd met during orientation week freshman year. Except for the time she and you went to second base, out of best-friend curiosity the night before you left to backpack around Europe, she has never, you assume, had eyes for anyone but Thad.

When you saw her profile on the reunion website, you weren't terribly surprised by anything. Even back at that Halloween you could see that she was tied to Thad—that she would someday convert to his faith, Judaism, and work in his parents' phone store. Then you scrolled down to the photo of one of their three sons and the breath was knocked out of you. This image of a boy, probably eight or nine years old, was the exact copy of Julia's younger brother, Kirk, who'd been killed in a drunk driving accident. It wasn't really an accident; Kirk and his best friend were extremely drunk and crashed head-on into a six-foot wide oak tree. From time to time you think of him and what a waste it was. Not only of his life but of Julia's. After he was killed, Julia quit acting and singing and seemed to let Thad take over. You always thought Thad was below her in talent, ambition, and looks. But he was sweet and a comfort to Julia after the funeral and in the subsequent months that was enough for her parents. You think of Kirk, in fact, more than Julia these days. There is a t-shirt of the 1990 Soccer World Cup in your dresser, second drawer, at home. A couple of weeks before he was killed you were at their parents' house, which was a kind of home away from home for you in high school. It was the end of summer break from college and you'd gone over to see Julia one last time. She was busy packing or something, so you and Kirk started playing soccer in the basement. You didn't want to get your shirt all messed up, so he lent you one of his favorites. Now it is completely threadbare (your wife loved how soft it is and wore it around the house), and you know you shouldn't keep the shirt because you look at it more than you should. You're not sure what it reminds you of—Kirk, Julia, your wife, or the four or five times you've gotten behind the wheel drunk. In any case, it's one of the profound sadnesses you feel from time to time that never really lets you go.

There she is standing underneath gold and brown balloons at the welcome table. Before you're even close enough, "Julia," you say, "Julia, over here." She turns her head and gives you a big, broad smile. They used to call her *Lips, Hips, and Teeth* and she's still all that, now with eyeglasses. She embraces you with a tight hold and you reciprocate. You both laugh out of the sheer joy of recognition.

"My God," she says, pushing you away. "You look good!"

You can tell she means it.

Her photo on the website was a headshot. When you embrace again (once wasn't enough) you look down to see how wide those hips have gotten.

"I'm sorry you didn't come to the football game last night. Our Eagles lost, but a lot of folks were there, already catching up."

"I'm sorry," you say, "our flight got in late."

"Well, no matter, we'll have time to visit," she says. "But not now. I have so much to do yet."

"Later's fine."

"And my parents are here—Hank's running the roulette table and Barb's helping with the food." She waves one hand in the direction of the cafeteria while the other is digging through a large box of junk. "You should go see them."

"I will for sure."

"Just so you know," she says, "they divorced ten years ago. They still have their ups and downs. It's one of their downs right now, I think. It's hard to keep track."

"Is there something in there I can help you find?"

"Nope, found it," she says, and hands you a button.

It's faded to a light pink color but the letters are still perfectly legible: *Happy Birthday, Scratch!* She made the button for you when you turned sixteen. There's a drawing of you, before you had eyeglasses, underneath the letters.

"Does anyone still call you Scratch?"

"No one ever did except you, Julia."

"Good."

"I've got to go back out to the car. Thad's here somewhere, still looks the same. He'll be happy to see you—one of the few faces he'll know."

"I'll find him."

"By the way," she says, "where's your wife? You've been hiding her—I didn't see any pictures on the website."

For a brief moment you think of telling Julia, then reject the idea.

"She's waiting until the little one is in bed," you say. "She'll be here later."

You're sure she knows you're lying.

"Can't wait to meet her," she says, and then hands you a cassette tape. "It's one of the mix tapes you made me."

"I'm not sure I even have something to play this on."

"You'll figure it out," she says.

Other people are waiting now. You tell her that you haven't paid for your entrance ticket yet. She sends you down the hall to the second welcome table which is at the entrance to the cafeteria. "I'll see you soon!" she says.

You're halfway to the cafeteria when you remember something you wanted to ask her. By the time you get back, she is talking with one of your classmates. It's someone you and Julia never liked, though now they look like old friends, like you and Julia must have a few minutes ago. You stand there, off to the side, waiting politely. You can't hear exactly what they're saying, but they're laughing and enjoying each other. After a couple of minutes, you turn to leave but Julia notices and reaches over for your arm, missing it though you feel the rush of air. You keep walking. You've forgotten what it was you wanted to say.

You line up at the second table. While you wait you peek into the cafeteria. A handful of people are around the refreshments table and a few others are milling about. This looks to be a bust. Is there even a quorum? Most people look as if they've swallowed their former selves. It starts to sink in that you're going to have to talk to a lot of classmates you never did before. And to their spouses.

A small procession rushes past you. There is Debbie Gerlich, short and loud and still oddly cute, in jeans and a designer t-shirt. There is Nina Wolf, still 6'1", wearing heels and a blouse that looks like it's made entirely of glitter. There is Rob Martinez who showed you his dad's hidden collection of *Playboys* when you were in middle school. There is Brian Stanic in blue and white Hawaiian shorts. There is Nancy Finch who looks nothing like the photo she posted on the website. There is Linda Brown who posted a long description of her life for the past twenty years but posted only photos of her two children, none of herself. And then there is Jason Fieldman who sees you and heads your way.

From the website you remember that he is a professor of sports education somewhere in Kentucky. He gives you a big smile and shakes your hand so hard that you are pulled out of line.

"Good to see you, Jason."

He immediately launches into a story about being on the same baseball team as kids. "And I was his catcher," he says to his wife.

"His who?" she says.

"He pitched, and I was his catcher. He had a great arm."

You don't know why he's talking to you in the third person, but it sounds both right and wrong.

"We were ten years old," you tell her.

"I know," he says, "but you were great."

"Your dad was the coach, wasn't he?"

"Right. Man, your arm was great—you should have kept with it."

"Thanks," you say, "but I remember they only let us pitch for three innings in little league."

"But that arm," he says and pats you on the shoulder, "damn fine arm."

You soon realize that you two have nothing left to say, unless one of you invents something. Fortunately, another classmate, one you don't quite recognize, whisks Jason and his wife away but not before he can give you another pat on the arm.

You turn back to the table to find Jackie Shimko staring at you.

"I recognized you right away," she says.

"You look wonderful."

"You too," she says. "Did you come from far away?"

"New Orleans."

"Oh, good grief. I mean, how it is down there? Were you there before Katrina? I went years ago on a college road trip for Mardi Gras. I don't remember much but...."

Ah, the same old Jackie. She was a popular girl in high school, the kind you wanted to see naked and possibly sleep with. One time you did get to see her breasts in the chemistry lab (she bent down to clean up a shattered beaker); her chest was as flat as Julia's hips were wide. You never knew her very well, but she was always kind to you. She is not unattractive standing there next to her husband, you assume, and donning an adult version of a little girl's princess dress, all white, pale pink, and delicate ruffle.

She goes on a little too long about New Orleans, but you're used to it. People always want to talk to you about what tragic devastation in the Third World is really like. When she finishes, you pay her for your ticket and say, "How many are coming tonight?"

"I've got 127 name tags," she says, spreading out her arms over the table. "About eighty classmates and the rest are spouses or partners."

"Twenty-five," a man in a pinstripe suit says. "Give or take. That's my estimate of how many single women will be here."

"Pardon me?"

"I could see," he says, pointing to his forehead, "you're doing the math. The number might be higher—if you count some of the wives. I'm sure a lot of husbands just brought them as props."

Either Jackie doesn't hear the man or pretends not to hear him. "Here you go, gentlemen," and she hands each of you a name tag. You look at your tag but don't recognize the name. She's mixed them up.

"God, I'm sorry," he says, and trades tags with you. "You're not who I thought you were."

"I feel that way about myself sometimes," you say.

"I apologize for…well, I didn't mean anything by the husband comment."

You don't quite understand what he means, but you tell him not to worry about it. He walks away in a hurry.

"Somewhere to get to, I guess." Jackie says.

You nod.

"I almost forgot," she says, "take this." She hands you an envelope. "It's for the auction at the end of the night. Just like we had for post-prom—you remember?"

"Of course," you say, though you aren't sure what she is talking about.

"Julia and I are really proud of this. There's a ton of stuff—most of it donated just like we did for the prom—matching mountain bikes, widescreen TV, gift certificates. We even got a few hermit crabs and goldfish."

"Goldfish?"

"You know, for the kids."

"Kids?"

"People's kids, you know, to take home."

"Right."

"And we saved the best for last—a weekend getaway to Suriname. Doesn't that sound romantic?"

You nod vigorously.

"It's so good to see you," she says, and gives you hug as if you were her prince. You thank her for all the hard work in organizing the reunion, and then someone else interjects: "Jackie!" It's your cue to move on.

You step into the cafeteria. The first thing you see is a large man in his sixties, with his arm around Sally Foster. They are having their photo taken by a man (Sally's husband?) with a tan the color of a spoiled orange. When the large man turns you see it's Conrad Clemmens, the old Dean of Students and assistant cross-country coach. You and Alex liked to call him Conrad though he insisted on being called Dean Clemmens. Sally was a wild child in high school, always in his office for one thing or another. Conrad's arm is now groping around Sally's waist. Maybe you should back out of this scene right now.

But to where?

On the left is the kitchen area where there is a long row of tables of food you can already tell you don't want to eat. On the right is the commons area which looks freakishly reminiscent of senior prom: shiny gold and brown streamers and enormous dice and playing cards hanging from the ceiling. It's coming back to you. May 1988 was smack in the middle of the initial rage of Mothers Against Drunk Driving, and the moms (and dads) in your high school took it seriously. That is how the idea of Las Vegas Night was born, or at least adopted from another local high school. Instead of crazy, triple-kegger post-prom parties, the parents of the senior class rented roulette wheels, blackjack tables, poker tables, and slot machines. After the dinner and dance at some overpriced venue, everyone came back to the school. At the door a parent handed you an envelope with a couple of thousand in play money and then directed you to the commons. It was lit up like a casino. Parents were all in position as croupiers or stationed at tables of food and non-alcoholic drinks.

You look inside the envelope now. Sure enough there's a small stack of play money. And this time, straight ahead of you, there's a bar with booze.

"When does Vegas start up?" you ask the guy behind the bar.

"Thing's quite classic, isn't it," he says in a vaguely British accent, "I saw the old folks arrive earlier. They're all in the kitchen getting arse-over-tit before manning the tables."

"But what time?"

"Right, sorry. I believe eight o'clock," he says and points to your hand. "You've got the schedule there, mate." In addition to the money in the envelope, there's a list of attendees and a schedule:

Cornfields have become strip malls,
Classmates have become grown-ups…(OK, maybe not all of them)

80's FLASHBACK REUNION PARTY!

WHEN!	WHAT!	WHERE!
7 – midnight	Food & Drink	Cafeteria
8 – 9pm	Slide Show	Auditorium
8 –11pm	Las Vegas Night!	Commons
8 – 11pm	Hawaiian Dance	Fieldhouse
11pm	Auction	Commons

Before you can wonder much about why there's an Englishman tending bar at an American high school reunion, he has taken off. Guess he wasn't the bartender after all. There are loads of bottles of gin, vodka, bourbon.

A couple comes up to the table next to you, and you quickly recognize the man. In high school, he was a nerd and a member of the gifted program. He wasn't in your immediate clique, but you two always got on very well. "Bob," you say, "how in the hell are you?"

He's as enthused as you are, and he quickly introduces his wife.

"We got married only last year," she says.

And he adds, "It was on one of my trips to China. I've been helping the Chinese with patents."

"The Kenyans and Brazilians, too," she says.

Bob and his wife both speak unpretentiously, and he strikes you as he always did: a super intelligent guy and a gentle soul.

"Tell him about your new firm," she says.

And so Bob tells a story of working for a high-powered law firm in Boston for almost ten years, and then just this past year setting out on his own.

"I actually do a lot of pro bono work," he says. "But that's okay, I enjoy the travel. Last year was my first walk along the Great Wall."

You tell him about your job and they both seem genuine in their interest. She then tells a story about one of their hobbies—magic tricks—and how sometimes they perform at a Cambridge pub. You picture the two of them on stage: Bob wearing a velvet cape and sawing his wife in half. It's completely campy, but it's also very sweet. They are an awkwardly cool couple. Except for your wife's funeral, this is the most socializing you've done in a very long time. And you don't notice, until Bob suggests a drink, that no one has been tending bar the entire time.

The three of you study the rows of booze. "Do you think," Bob's wife says, "that the bottle of absinthe really has wormwood in it?"

"I like your style," you say.

Fortunately they seem to ignore your moronic comment.

"How about gin and tonics?" Bob says.

Bob cuts limes, his wife opens a fresh bottle of gin, and you offer to go back around the table to get the ice. It all fits together smoothly, like the conversation itself, until you clink plastic cups. At that moment Bob sees another classmate—someone you never knew very well—and chit-chat ensues. Despite Bob's wife smiling at you from time to time, you're soon quietly cut out of the conversation. It's not intentional, it's just how things go. So you begin cutting lime wedges and filling other classmates' drink orders.

After five minutes, Bob and his wife have drifted away and you've earned a few bucks in tips. Then, there's a gap and you can make yourself another drink. After two failed efforts at making a decent Manhattan, you are stopped by someone slapping a hand on the table.

"Martinis!"

You think you recognize the man and then it quickly passes. Instead of just making the drinks, you say, "I don't work here. I mean, I could make that for you, but maybe I shouldn't."

"Why not?" he says. "Hey, aren't you—wait, it's coming to me—I've got your face, can't get the name... starts with an 'm'...Mike or Matt or...dude, just give me a glass and I'll get it."

The guy already seems inebriated. You hand him a glass anyway. Then he remembers your last name, but mispronounces it.

You correct him: "Rhymes with *jock-itch*."

"Yeah, I remember now," he says. "I'm Kilroy, Daniel Kilroy. Actually I used to go by Danny, but I've dropped that. Call me Kilroy. You remember me?"

"I remember your face, I think."

"Yeah," he says, "I used to be scrawny, used to get beat-up a lot."

This is hard to imagine. He's well over six-foot and rough looking. His jaw is square to the point of being boxy, and now that you are getting a good look, one eye is brown and one blue. But the fact is you don't remember him at all. You admit this to him, adding that you're sorry he used to get picked on.

"Doesn't matter," Kilroy says, "that all ended after I joined the Merchant Marines. I grew balls fast." He rolls up his shirt-sleeve and shows you a tattoo of an anchor with a snake wrapped around it. Something is written in script underneath.

"Don't read on me?"

"Don't *tread* on me, man," he says.

"Oh."

"Look," he says, "there's that rain." He points to a woman with dirty blonde hair standing alone by the buffet.

"Rain?"

"Raina, I said, Raina—that's her name. I heard she used to

be a marine and now's a cop. Nothing hotter than a chick with a piece on her hip."

You've never given it much thought; most of your fantasies have involved your wife in an off-white nurse's outfit or a tennis skirt. But maybe Kilroy's right. His arm is still gesturing toward her. You try to imagine this woman in a police hat and handcuffs or straddling a police motorcycle. "I don't know," you say. Trying not to offend him, you sweep your hand in front of your face trying to brush away a waft of someone's perfume. "I'm not getting the attraction."

"Think of the gun," he says, "and the bullets."

You picture a gun, but she's not holding it—you are. You picture when you held one in your hands for the first time last year. The Professor convinced you to go to the firing range. Unload some psycho-ballast, were his words. Since your son would be at a playdate all afternoon and a trip to the range would get you out of grading papers, you acquiesced. On the drive it looked as though it would rain hard. No time to get The Professor's semi-automatic rifle from storage, you'd just have to use his ex-wife's subcompact Glock. By the time you bought ammo and got out there, it was raining and the range was nearly empty. Holding a gun for the first time, you thought you'd feel your mortality. But you had a hard time cocking the thing and this made you feel clumsy and weak. The Professor had to show you how to pull back the slide while pushing forward with the grip.

You have no idea why, but suddenly you're telling him about the firing range, how shooting a hundred and twenty rounds was supposed to release stress, how you didn't really enjoy the whole experience.

"I've only fired a gun one time," he says, still eyeing the woman who seems to be picking something out of her potato or macaroni salad with her fingers. "But I'd fire one into her."

He guffaws.

This strikes you as strange—Kilroy looks exactly like the type of guy who's got an arsenal in the back of his pickup. But this whole discussion is very odd anyway, and you wonder if the rest of the evening's conversations will be as odd.

"Were you afraid of it?" he asks.

"What?"

"The gun, man, the gun."

"Not really."

"That's the problem. You gotta try doing something you're afraid of—you have a fear of heights, maybe? Try climbing a telephone pole, sit on top of your chimney, try kissing the sun."

How drunk is this guy?

You look back in the direction of the woman but she's not there. Another woman, who looks either Hawaiian or Japanese, comes up and puts her arms around Kilroy's waist. A couple behind them makes sighing noises.

"Hold your horses," Kilroy tells them and waves his hand.

The couple obeys.

"This is my awesome wife, Roz," he says, "so much better than the first psycho bitch I was married to."

She smiles.

He's already made one martini and is halfway through it. You ask his wife if she would like her martini dirty.

"Mail-order bride, dude," he says. "She doesn't speak much English."

You thought they all came from Russia.

"Olives?" you ask, shaking a jar.

She nods in a way that could mean yes or no. But then she says, "He's messing with you."

"Forget the olives, Jockitch," he says. "You want to hit the craps table with us?"

"As long as I'm back here," you say, "I might as well tend bar a while."

"Suit yourself," Kilroy says.

"It was nice to meet you," his wife says.

Thank god you've always been quick with the excuses. The couple behind them puts in an order, and a line starts to form. You lose track of the dirty blonde who was picking at her potato or macaroni salad. You pour drinks for another fifteen minutes and make five dollars in tips. Finally a parent comes over to relieve you. It's Mr. Phillips, the father of your oldest neighborhood friend, Rick Phillips. Mr. Phillips was, or still is, an electronic engineer like your father. After introducing yourself, he recognizes you. He says his son just arrived and he points across the room. The last time you saw Rick was nearly fifteen years ago. You were driving through Albuquerque and spent the night at his place. He had recently married a divorcée with a young son, and he had taken a job as a research scientist at Sandia Laboratory, a sister facility to Los Alamos. Already he had secret clearance and couldn't tell you anything about his work.

"Nothing?" you said.

"I can tell you this," he said casually, "I'm working on a way to make bombs lay down better."

"Better?"

"So that the destruction quotient is higher."

Part of you was happy that he couldn't tell you more.

You and Rick see each other at the same time. You walk over but aren't sure how to greet him—a regular business-type handshake, an overhand pickup-basketball handshake, or some kind of handshake/hug combo. He was, after all, your best friend growing up—until the last two years of high school when he fell in with a more popular crowd. At the last minute you decide to follow his lead: It's a vigorous regular handshake accompanied by a few awkward *I-can't-believe-how-long-it's-beens*. After the inquiries about each other's wives and kids, you ask if he still works at Sandia.

"Sure," he says, "after 9-11, things picked up a lot. Before that, we were in a bit of a slump...after the Soviets imploded... well, it wasn't a happy time. But now we're back in business."

The two of you talk about how Algonquin has changed, how it was difficult to find the high school among the shopping centers, new stoplights, and subdivisions. Then he says, "I never really fit here in the Midwest. The first time I went to California for that NASA internship, I fell in love with the ocean and the mountains."

He continues a small sermon on the outdoors of New Mexico, and although you agree that it has a stunning terrain, you steer the conversation back around to his job at Sandia.

"There was a time, it's true," he says, "when I thought of leaving the lab for commercial airline work. But I'll never leave now. The work is challenging, I have a lot to do, and am in charge of a couple of big projects."

He goes on in more generalities. You notice he's wearing pressed slacks with a crease, and he seems more stiff than you remember, not only in physical appearance—he obviously still hits the gym—but in demeanor. This is the same guy who used to smoke pot before school three times a week. You swallow the rest of your drink. It's your second and the buzz is kicking in. You feel like pressing him, for no other reason than you'll likely not see him again for another fifteen years.

"What about your son?"

"What do you mean?"

"What does he think about Dad making things that kill people?"

His face goes flush but the features remain composed. "I don't see it that way," he says.

"I'm sorry," you say, "that came out wrong."

"No, it's okay," he says, "I get that question sometimes, maybe not as boldly as that but still. We always were smart asses in school, weren't we? To answer your question, I see my work as defensive."

"How's that?"

"I'm sure you've heard the argument—the best defense is a strong offense. I don't quite believe it. But I also don't think there's a way around being on either the defense or the offense. You can't simply sit on the sidelines."

For a second you think he's actually talking about football.

"That reminds me," you say, "of Don DeLillo's novel *White Noise*. I taught it last spring along with *Hamlet*, *Huck Finn*, *The Sound and The Fury*. Part of my 'Dead White Men' course—no matter DeLillo isn't dead yet—none of my students knew the difference. And well, I only taught the course because I'd never actually read any of the books before. They were all good, except for Faulkner who's way out of my league...." You realize you've forgotten the point you wanted to make.

"I only read nonfiction," Rick says, "science and history."

"Oh yes, I remember now," you say. "There's this part near the end of *White Noise* where a character talks about the two kinds of people in the world: diers and killers. Diers simply wait for death to happen to them, but killers fight against death by causing other people's deaths—"

"Killing them, you mean."

"Yes, exactly. By killing, killers store up a kind of mental mettle against death as well as...I guess my point is...what if one doesn't want to play the game—offense or defense—or wants to play another game, like solitaire?"

"I don't think there is such a thing as solitaire. It's an illusion. You're still playing against yourself. There's still an offense and defense."

"I thought dialectics went out of fashion a century or two ago."

"I don't know who the dialectics were," he says, "I'm a plain and simple Darwinian. To survive you have to evolve—to create better and more adaptive strategies than others. Like with the Russians—in the end they weren't just fascists, they were wimps."

He takes a slug from his beer and looks around the room.

"What about Sting?"

"Who?"

"Sting's song about the Russians loving their children too."

"I'm sure they did."

You wonder if he really believes this. Back in fourth grade he once called you a "Jew bastard," which wasn't true because you aren't Jewish, though the bastard part could be true—being adopted it's most likely that you were born out of wedlock. When he called you that name, your knee-jerk reply was to yell "Heil Hitler!" and give him the Nazi salute. Not long after the event you and Rick made up—both of you ignorant of the Holocaust and what you were really saying—but later in college you began to regret what you did, even if it was by a nine-year-old. It was in college, too, that you began to wonder if you could be Jewish—you have the nose and perhaps even the desire.

Then the thought just comes out of your mouth: "I've always wanted to be Jewish."

"What are you talking about?"

"Okay," you say, "Jewish just for a week or a month or something. Jews always seem so special. My wife is Jewish, but she didn't really grow up Jewish. Her father was a quasi-Communist, actually. Best friends with Abbie Hoffman for a while."

Before you know it you've gone into a story about how your father-in-law and Abbie once started a shop in the East Village which sold crafts and items made by rural Southerners, and how the friendship disintegrated when Abbie wanted to give all the inventory away instead of selling it. There's more to the story, but it ends with your father-in-law buying a lifetime subscription to the *Wall Street Journal*.

"I've been getting the *Journal* for years," Rick says. "Didn't know they had a lifetime subscription—how much?"

"No idea. Maybe it's just a New York thing."

"Was he in New York?"

"What?"

"When the planes hit," Rick says. "I was at the Pentagon."

"Pentagon?"

"During the attacks."

"Jesus."

"Well, the week before them, but close enough."

He starts talking about how Syria is more lethal than Iran and how terrorism might be the best thing that happened to the country: "Get people to take things seriously again." While he is worrying about the future of the presidency, you feel your buzz slipping away. You no longer care about the specifics of whatever top-secret project he is working on.

He asks for your opinion about the upcoming election. You dodge the question. Something inside of you feels sad not only because you want to escape him, but because he probably feels the same way about you.

"The slide show," you interrupt, "I almost forgot about it."

"I'll go with you," he says. "My wife went back to the hotel for something. She'll call when she wants me."

The program has already started. There are about fifty people in the auditorium. You and Rick slip in on the side. You immediately recognize the voice narrating the image on the screen: Dave Denton. It's amazing how fast a wave of memories hits you. Dave was a smart ass in high school, much like yourself, but he was part of the popular crowd. You remember he always wore argyle sweaters with matching socks.

On the screen is an image of four sour-faced basketball players sitting on the bench. Dave is talking about how he used to be the butt of a joke senior year. The guys in the photo were the best players, but coach benched them for half the season. Dave can't remember why. "In any case," he says, "I was pretty excitable during our games. And even though they did this to me just about every game, I still fell for it. Either Jason or Tony would turn to me and say *Dave, Dave, coach is calling you*! I'd stand up, run down to coach, and crouch down next to him waiting for his instructions. After a few seconds, coach would ask me what the hell I wanted. I'd turn around and Jason and Tony would be laughing hysterically."

Next up is a photo of Dave and his high school girlfriend, Mary Gooding, at homecoming. You have little recollection of her; so much for your stellar memory. A man kneels in front of Dave and a flash goes off; it must be the photographer documenting the reunion. Now he takes a shot of the screen. Somehow that strikes you as redundant.

Dave shuttles through more images of homecoming—the band, the dance. It's uninteresting, as the pictures are all of him. Suddenly, Rick needles you in the arm, "Hey, look who's over there?" He motions with his head. You glance around the auditorium, seeing a few familiar faces, or rather backs of heads and profiles. "No, that way," Rick says, and points. Then you see her clearly—the woman you didn't expect to make the trip all the way from Arizona: Lane Wilson. You almost forgot about her. Really you did. It's not suppression of bad memories, though there were plenty of those after she left you for a previous boyfriend, an abusive dimwit.

You used to call her "Angel." An appropriate nickname; she was your first love, after all, even if sometimes she was dense. Once, for example, she thought you were choking on a tortilla chip in the lunchroom. You pushed her away and said the pop had simply gone down the wrong pipe. "That happens to me," she said, "the pop sometimes goes down the hole for solids instead of the one for liquids." After a couple of drawings on scrap paper, you still couldn't convince her that one hole is for food and the other is for air and that food, solid or liquid, goes down the same hole. You should have asked her what happens to things that are part solid, part liquid, like ice cream with nuts or beef stew.

Now it's the senior prom on the screen, conveniently marking the end of your first love.

She wore a sleeveless pink chiffon dress and you donned a white tuxedo with pink bowtie and cummerbund. You always thought that you two shared a singular connection, which other couples couldn't have, because both of you were adopted. But you didn't have that great of a connection. When she broke your heart it felt like each of those couple of hundred snowballs you threw at a lamppost one bitter-cold March midnight, a handful of them smashing against the hard bulb of light, none ever coming close to breaking it. And now there she is, sitting less than thirty feet away in a cobalt blue dress. Lane Snyder née Wilson, who according to her update on the website, is the mother of four, including twins Quinn and Mattie. What are you going to do about her just sitting there?

You raise your hand to your face, as if the scent of her on

your middle finger circa 1987 still lingers. The first time your finger parted her labia was at a church lock-in—she let you put an index finger inside her and moved it around a little. After about ten minutes, your hand started to cramp but you kept going. Suddenly she pulled your finger away (you thought it might be hurting her) and rolled on top of you, slowly plunging down her moist vulva (as you had been taught to call it by your mother as a child) onto your underwear hard-on. It only lasted a minute or two before she climbed off you. She did leave a nice wet mark. This was the closest you ever got to intercourse with Lane, which was infuriating at the time but ultimately for the best. Later as a college freshman you would lose your virginity to your second love, a junior nursing major who was incredibly sweet and performed a nightly fellatio on you which has never been rivaled. Still, you blame Lane for ruining your second love: Lane broke you and you knew even before meeting your second love that you would break her. It was probably Lane's legs that did it: she had once-in-a-lifetime legs and sitting up in your seat, looking over at them now they still appear decent. And yet you're not really interested in peeking up her skirt anymore.

You turn back to the screen. It's a collage of images of guys golfing. Dave starts telling a story about a golf tournament in which he came in third. Suddenly a voice bellows from behind you: "Dude, what the hell is this—golf isn't even a sport!"

You almost recognize the voice, even if it sounds somewhat drunk. But Dave ignores it and continues his story for another sentence, until the voice interrupts: "Not a sport, dude!"

Dave turns around and shields the light projector with his hand. He's trying to see to the back. "Tony, is that you? Good one."

"No, dude, it ain't Tony, and like I said golf blows!"

"That's your opinion," Dave says, with more composure

than you think possible, "but I happen to enjoy it. You don't have to watch if you don't—"

"Dude, this is your representation of what happened in high school. It's so biased."

There's some grumbling in the audience. A couple of men stand up in front, Dave's old friends—members of the basketball team, it looks like from their height. One of them raises a fist. Excellent, a fight. This might liven things up. The audience seems poised.

"Sit down, gentlemen," Dave says, gesturing with both arms. He turns back to the voice in the shadows. "Sir, yes, I completely agree with you. This is my version of high school. I can't help that. I didn't do any research, write up a questionnaire, if that's your idea. Though I am a golf pro at the country club in town.... But now that I think of it—do you have any photos you'd like to show us? Have you prepared a presentation as I have?"

Some people are looking forward at Dave and some are turned around in their seats, craning their necks. You don't know why the lights haven't been brought up yet. Then from the shadows a large figure walks down the center aisle. He's got both hands in the air, as in "don't shoot."

"Jason Fieldman," Dave says, "you sorry son-of-a-gun."

"And you pretentious old fart," Jason says.

Front and center the two men give each other man-slaps on the back and their other friends start doing high-fives.

"People," Jason says, "isn't Dave Denton something else? It's been a few years since I've seen him...but a fucking powerpoint presentation! I love this guy."

Rick turns to you and rolls his eyes. "Let's go," he whispers.

You don't really want to stay, but you worry about having to hang out with Rick for the rest of the night. It's sad—this is not how you expected to feel about him.

He's getting up to leave. "Coming?"

"I'd like to see how this mess turns out," you say.

Dave and company look like they are about to sing the school fight song on stage. You look over at Lane and notice her husband this time. You recognize him. He was the guy she started dating as soon as she got to Arizona State. You met him during Christmas break that first year of college. He had a two-letter name, like TJ or DJ or TD, and something was wrong with his hand, birth defect, you felt awkward shaking the deformed thing. He was a nice guy—you do recall that. But his hand gets you thinking again about her...the first time she let you stick your hand up her shirt as you were parked in her parents' driveway. It's a nice memory, but what good are another few paragraphs of that going to get you?

You decide you could use another drink and quietly leave the auditorium. If you see Rick again, you'll have to invent an ending for Dave Denton's version of high school.

6.

Sitting in a stall in the men's room, you swallow both martinis—the one Mr. Phillips poured for you and the one he poured for your wife who, even if alive, would neither have wanted to attend this shindig nor ordered a martini; she preferred bourbon when things got tough. Since you traveled all this way and twenty years to see these people, you start thinking something better come of it.

Stepping out of the men's room a few minutes later, you notice old folks standing behind tables in the commons and wonder how much they envy the young before them who are not so young anymore. Aging well, it occurs to you, seems to be about learning how to envy less.

You spy Julia's dad, Hank. He's a broad-shouldered man, played linebacker or something for Wisconsin. You remember him as a beer-loving teddy bear of a guy, fatherly in a brotherly sort of way.

You walk over and stand in front of his table.

"What's your lucky number, son?" he says, though his head is pointed down; he's cleaning up a spilt drink.

"How about *scratch me*?"

He looks up. "Holy hell, Jockitch! Jules said you might be here."

Hank reaches over the table and gives you a crushing hug. He's truly happy to see you. Or, he's already drunk. It's beginning to feel like heroic drinking is the only way people are going to endure the evening.

"You got money?" he says, "I can slip you more if you need it. Go ahead, play some numbers."

Before you know it, you've laid down a few hundred here and there and a few spins of the wheel have taken them away.

"Ach," Hank says, "gambling, who can tell?"

"I've always heard that gamblers—real gamblers—don't play to win, they play to lose."

"Sounds about right," he says. "You see Barb yet? She'll be glad to see you."

You say you're sorry about Barb and him splitting up. He tells you how Kirk's death took its toll, how he didn't want the divorce, etc. But he assures you that his ex-wife and he are still the best of friends. You don't know where to take the conversation from there—the only thing that comes to mind is the t-shirt.

"I got him that shirt," Hank says, "that was a great World Cup. I don't watch soccer anymore, can't bear it, but I've still got my German blood. I follow the games in the paper. Boy, Barb would really like to hear about that shirt."

Before you have a chance to go tell her, Hank explains how no one has been to the roulette table, except for you, in the last half hour and no one will for a while—the dance is about to start up. He asks if you'd take over for a while. Thinking he has to use the bathroom, you agree.

"Sometimes one has to be forthright," he says, "convicted."

Does he mean *convinced*?

"I hear you," you say, and remember how much your wife hated that turn of phrase.

"Thanks," he says. "I'll see you a little later."

He heads off in the direction of the food tables and you realize he's going to visit Barb instead of the men's room.

"Play to lose!" you yell after him.

You spin the wheel, laying bets down on your wife's and son's birthdays. Nothing. You try your own birthday. Then your mother's, father's, sister's. No luck. Roulette is ridiculous.

It's been at least ten minutes—what's Hank doing over there? A couple you don't recognize wants to play. One of them wins five hundred on the first spin. If it were you, you'd keep betting, but they walk away in giddiness. As soon as they're gone, Kilroy and his wife sit down.

"Dude, are you working all the rides tonight?"

"Looks that way."

"Roz, slide two hundred onto lucky thirteen over there."

You spin the wheel. Red 12.

"Another two hundred, babe, on thirteen."

Kilroy plays the same three more times and loses two thousand fake dollars. "You ain't bringing me any luck with that spin." Roz suggests moving to the blackjack table. "No," he says, "I'm having fun here with my old buddy, Jockitch. You really don't remember me at all?"

Again you tell him that his face does look familiar.

"I'm going for more drinks," says Roz.

"Yeah, sure," he says, still looking you in the eye. "I remember you."

You simply can't bring up any images of him in high school. This is getting a little creepy. But you aren't afraid of him, despite the tattoo; you remember who your enemies were and he wasn't one of them.

"You dated Kelly Campbell, that track star babe."

You didn't really date her. You had a brief interlude a few years after high school graduation. Kilroy can't possibly know about that; no one knows about that besides you and her.

"No," you say, "I dated Lane-the-Pain in high school."

"Who? No, that's not right," he says, "it was Kelly Campbell."

"Dude," you say, trying to put it in a language he will understand, "I think I'd remember slipping my salami between Kelly Campbell's steak knives."

"I'll pretend I didn't hear that," Kelly says.

You literally gasp for air. Kelly and Jake Jones, her high school boyfriend who now looks to be her husband, are standing at the end of the table.

"I was just messing with you," Kilroy says.

"Not funny," Jake says. He may have lost some hair, but he's the same studly Jake Jones, captain of the track team, all-state pole vaulter. What you would have given to have had his physique. And to have known what's between those steak knives. Kelly steps into the light and yes, she's still pretty, a well-preserved pretty. Never mind what society says, you've never liked the nubile schoolgirl (part of the reason you became a high school teacher); for as long as a boy can remember you have always been attracted to middle-aged pretty.

"You gonna spin that thing," Jake says.

"Story of my life," you say, not knowing what you mean.

Another couple has joined the table and everyone lays down bets. You are set to spin but notice a problem.

"Does anyone see the ball?"

After a brief hunt, Kelly says, "Right there," and points in the direction of your fly. The ball is sitting next to your drink on the table.

"Sorry folks."

"I was going to offer one of my balls," Kilroy says.

No one laughs.

You spin the wheel and drop the ball in. Black 22. Everyone loses. Stupid game. What are you supposed to do with all the money the house has won? Where the hell is Hank?

"There's a strategy to roulette," Kilroy says.

"Well, you certainly don't know it," Roz says, setting down a drink in front of him.

"If you bet on red all the time," Jake says, "you're bound to win at some point. You just have to have enough money to keep going."

"Very wise," Kilroy says, "but not very true."

"Care to bet on that," Jake says, and holds up a couple of hundreds.

"Oh please," Kelly says. "I'm getting a drink."

"I'm getting drunk," you say. She smiles and heads off in the same direction Hank did.

"Anyone care to man this thing?" you ask. "I'm just filling in for Mr. Baumholder."

Roz takes the ball from the wheel.

"Thanks," you say.

Before you can go find steak knives, Kilroy takes your arm and whispers, "How about a smoke outside?"

"I don't smoke."

"Joints, I mean, I have a couple."

"Pot doesn't do it for me."

"Kelly Campbell does?"

You tell him you'll see him later and leave.

You check the refreshment and food tables and get stuck making small talk with random and forgettable classmates and their spouses. You mill around outside the bathrooms for ten minutes, receiving looks from people as if you're stalking a small child who's waiting for her daddy. You go to the field house to take a peek at the dance, where you talk to one interesting classmate who says she won the Illinois State Lottery five years ago and now lives in Reykjavik. "Iceland's beautiful and super cheap," she says, "everyone thinks Iceland is cold and barren and Greenland is lush and dense. It's actually the reverse." You wonder if you could move there; theoretically you could teach—the principal once told you—from anywhere. Just as you're about to ask the lottery winner about the education system in Iceland, her husband or partner or whoever—a small, unimpressive man—intervenes.

It's now almost ten o'clock, and all you have to show for this evening is a few business cards. You've wasted too much time looking for a woman with whom you made-out a few times and petted a little. In your mind you run over the history as if perhaps it's changed since the last time you've gone down this particular libidinal lane. It was your first year out of college. You were excited about having your first job, right in downtown Chicago. Because you couldn't afford to live in the city, you lived with your parents and commuted on the train. One morning about nine months into your now unexciting job, you saw Kelly running across the train tracks in heels, splashing coffee everywhere. In high school she had been a sprinter and you had been a miler. You and the other long-distance runners would watch her on the other side of the track—seemingly a world away—as she did warm-up stretches in royal blue running tights which highlighted her blue eyes and blonde hair. On the train platform, however, you didn't think twice about it: You walked right up to her and started talking. She turned out not to be who you thought she was. She was warm, funny, and smart. You two talked nonstop the entire hour commute into the city—that first day and every day afterwards for a month. At some point you kissed her which led to an overnight camping trip to the Indiana

Dunes where you both got too drunk, probably out of nerves, to do anything but pass out on top of each other. Technically she was still dating Jake, so after you moved away for grad school there were a few brief phone calls and messages and then everything faded away. All these years later no one could accuse you of carrying a torch for her; if anything it'd be a small box of matches which now and then you've opened up, taken one out, but never been able to light.

Kelly Campbell, you decide, is not who you've come here for.

You find an exit and step outside to get some air. A cool breeze and the smell of decomposing leaves, the sure tell of autumn; it's always been almost too visceral for you to handle. You start walking to the parking lot. On the way, you're stopped by the class clown, Joe Michalszewski. You didn't know him very well in high school, but he's pretty drunk and begins talking to you as if you two had been best friends.

"I worked as a stockbroker in Chicago for ten years," he says, "before being asked by the SEC to go do something else. I've been in sales ever since." He chucks you on the shoulder.

You try not to give him a look.

"Then in 2001," he says, "I got married to Amy, a clinical psychologist from Schaumburg. I guess," he laughs, "I'm kind of like her full time project."

You nod.

"We have two wonderful kids…."

Over the course of an endless five minutes, you nod a few more times. The way he talks makes you think he's going to drag you over to his car and try to sell you electronics out of the trunk.

Then he tells you that he's a motivational speaker on the side. You find this somewhat intriguing.

"It's all in how well you manage impromptu," he says, hiccups, and waves his hand like a magician.

"How's that?"

"You've got to move the scene forward, as they say."

"Who?"

"The actors. Improv. There's a strategy they use called *Hell yes...and moreover*. Easiest thing in the world to teach. Here, let me demonstrate." Joe adjusts his tie, brushes off his shoulders, and in between hiccups clears his throat.

You're not that intrigued. So you tell him there's somebody you promised to meet, but he doesn't seem to hear you.

"Look," he says, "I give you two words at random, like... chateau and...puke. What can you do with them?"

"Do?"

"Come on—improv! Hurry up, hurry up."

"I puked in your chateau."

"Good," he says, and chucks you on the shoulder again. You wonder if it'll bruise. "Now I say, *Hell yes* you puked and it was all over the place! *And moreover* your wife was running behind you, cleaning up after your shit."

"My wife's dead."

"There you go," he says, "*Hell yes*...she died of laughter the next morning when she showed you all the puke she'd collected in a bucket, *and moreover* you—"

"No, she really died," you say. "Last year."

"What?" he says.

You return his blank look.

"Oh shit," he says, as if you've tried to slap him out of his inebriation. "You're the guy..." he says, and then mumbles something about Kilroy.

Kilroy?

"Look," he says, "I mean...what I mean is...well, see how

that fits into the situation at hand?"

Situation? You don't know what to say. Is this another prompt?

"I'm sorry," he says, and puts his arm on your shoulder. He's close enough now that you can see he's got a thin red-wine mustache.

"*Hell yes*," you mumble.

"That's the spirit," he says. "Well, I'll be seeing you." He makes a move to leave then turns back. "You know I just might have the thing to cheer you up."

"I don't need cheering." You don't mean to say it in a sarcastic way but it maybe comes out so.

"No," he says, "I can see that."

"*And moreover…*" you try but can't finish the sentence.

"I'm sorry," he says, "that came out funny. I meant, well… here." He takes your hand, puts something hard into the palm, and closes it. You're almost afraid to see what's in there. Before you can say anything he's stumbled off between the cars. When you finally open your hand, you find a silver money clip stuffed with fake bills. Good lord. You jam it in your pocket and try to remember where you parked.

Maybe there's something you could use as disguise—a hat or sunglasses in your parents' car. They've always got enough junk in their car that a person could live out of it for a couple of weeks.

You pass by the same car you noticed on the way in—with the same guys listening to football on the radio. It's obvious to you now that these are husbands of classmates and that they've never gone into the building. Maybe it's better to stay outside.

"Who's playing?" you ask.

"USC and Ohio State," says a guy wearing a pink button-up.

"What's the score?"

"We're killing them, 28-3."

"We?"

"USC."

"You're kidding."

"Pardon me?"

"You must be from So Cal."

"Yeah," pink button-up says. He gestures toward the building. "Your wife in there too?"

"No."

"So you're a 'member of the class'," he says, making scare quotes.

"Right."

There's a blast from the radio.

"Aw, shit," says a guy in a suit and a Yankees baseball cap. "We just fucking fumbled."

Pink button-up turns back toward you. "How's it going in there?"

"Hard to tell."

The suit and baseball cap moans louder, sets down his beer, and turns toward you. "I'm Charles. Didn't catch your name?"

"Jockitch."

"What's that?"

"Sorry, that's what they called me in high school."

"So this is your school."

"Yeah."

"Sorry to hear it."

"It wasn't that bad."

"Okay."

Pink button-up offers you a beer from a cooler.

"That's all right, I have to get going."

"Take one to go."

"Thanks."

You're ten yards away when you realize it's a light beer. Too many bubbles and no taste. For no good reason, you feel like cocking back your arm, yelling *Go Ohio State!*, and throwing the can at them. But getting pummeled in the parking lot of your old high school isn't what you've come here for either. You set the beer down gently behind the tire of a car, the way you used to put ketchup packets behind the tire of the school bus; you knew you wouldn't get to witness the mini explosion, but the idea of it excited you.

In the car you feel like a cliché. You'd like to stare at rain hitting the windshield, pretend you're crying in the shower. Unfortunately it's not raining.

Under the front seats, you find the dried, blackened peels of two bananas, a few mugs with old tea bags, an ice scraper, wrapping paper, three gloves, a ski mask, and assorted balled-up dirty tissues which probably contain peach pits and apple cores. You're not even going to look in the trunk. Maybe you could walk back inside wearing the ski mask?

You don't want to walk by the football fans again, so you start walking the long way around the building. Tennis courts, soccer field, football field surrounded by the track. Except for the houses that have popped up where corn and soybeans used to be around the school, everything is where you left it twenty years ago.

7.

The walk and cool evening air do you some good. As soon as you find something to eat and drink, you'll be ready for round two. You enter the school from the same doors as before but this time you take the long way around to the cafeteria. You run into Julia, who is struggling with a large box through a side entrance. You take the box from her. Inside you see a lot of smaller wrapped boxes.

"What's this?"

"Gifts for the superlatives?"

"Superlatives?"

She pulls out one with a tag that reads "Most Changed."

You run the two words over in your head again and again until they don't even sound like English anymore. "You think I changed the most?" That doesn't sound right either.

"No, silly," Julia says, and takes it back. "I was just showing you an example."

Then you realize what this is about: senior superlatives. Best legs, best smile, biggest flirt, steadiest, peppiest, most helpful, most intelligent. You even think you see one in the box that reads "Bluest Eyes."

"What do you want me to do with them?"

"I've got to find Jackie to coordinate the auction. Could

you take these to the commons for me?"

"Of course."

"We'll get to talk yet," she says, "I promise!"

As you watch her hips make their way down the hall, you think about rankings. And this quickly leads to thoughts of your last girlfriend, the woman before your wife. She ranked everything—movies, restaurants, albums, books, colors. You never considered it before: Did she ever rank you sexually? You had an awful lot of sex with that woman—three years' worth—thousands of times in and out, in and out. Throughout twenty years of having sex, more or less steadily and regularly, there are certain moments that stand out. One time with serious girlfriend number 3, who you were engaged to for a month, complete with Tiffany diamond. It was her college graduation night: She was topside in a navy blue velvet bra still strapped on tightly, mounting you. Then at a precise moment of mutual-orgasm, she leaned back so far that her shoulder blades touched your knees. It was reckless, of course—felt like your penis was going to snap—but it was divine and never to be replicated. Even now thinking about it casually, you have a nice erection. How come she is not here? You'd like to see what she looks like, fifteen years since you mailed that ring back to Tiffany's in Chicago. (They still send you a catalogue once a year.) Why does it always boil down to looks, to how your penis might react? At one time you might have made love to Julia, but as you watch her behind vanish down the hallway, you know you wouldn't do it now. You're pathetic. As a teenager you thought it was only you who sized up every girl or woman with the thought *I'd do her / I'd not do her.* Then in college you realized that every young man has the same thought. Now that you're nearly forty, it is tedious and yet unavoidable that you still make the judgment the minute you see a woman—you're just not as conscious of it as you used to be. You'll be an old man at the fiftieth high school reunion (should there be such a sad venture), and you will be sizing up the sixty-eight-year-olds, wondering if there's a firm tit among them. Sometimes it'd be so much easier if you were gay; gay and Jewish for a day. Sounds like an absurdist musical someone might have put on in Auschwitz.

You're incorrigible. Then you decide you're pitiful. Finally you think the only word to describe you is a noun: *men*. You're like all the rest of them but you pretend to think you're better. And it's not a sobering thought, it's a boring one.

Set the box against the wall and sit down next to it.

Close your eyes.

Maybe you simply need to calm down—vipassana meditation-style, as The Professor showed you. Don't bother getting into yoga position, but keep your eyes closed and take even breaths. After a minute or two the body relaxes...

...but then the mind kicks in: Why all the serial monogamy (five two-year plus relationships) before you finally got married? The answer lies in your wife. She was always saying how compatible you two were—"I can't believe we found each other!"—as if you both had been buried treasures and now were sitting next to each other under a plaque in a museum for the married. You could and couldn't believe it: you did have a lot in common, but probably no more than any of your previous relationships. No, what it came down to was that each of you could adapt to new situations. You can't say you learned this through living with your father and his schizophrenia; it was more likely that all the running away from it—career changes, moves to new cities—shaped your ability to adapt. And then when you met your wife, her family's problems took up so much emotional space that there was no room for yours. But you didn't mind. Altruism seemed like a fine excuse to avoid home. Your wife, on the other hand, embraced her family's tragedy: Little Ma's cancer. Or rather she embraced her mother—adored her like you'd never witnessed before. (It is both the happiest and the saddest story you've never told.) That is, even if you don't like spending a lot of time with your mother, you will be hunched-over and broken when she dies—not because you will have loved her so much, but because you *should have* loved her better or deeper or more incomprehensibly. The tears of sorrow will be tears for yourself. But your wife wasn't any old "you": She was more in love with Little Ma than she was in love with you. In high school Little Ma said *Try out for the soccer team*—so she played soccer, though she would rather have joined the swimmers. *Read James Joyce*—so she read James Joyce, though she would rather have read Jane Austen. *Go to law school*—though she would have rather become a social worker. *Paint Owen's bedroom baby blue*, though you would have preferred yellow rose. And yet you knew all of this before getting married. It didn't bother you that much because there was your edge, your destiny, your trump card: You knew Little Ma's colon cancer was going to get her; she would die before you. That terrible day would come, and you would be the only true love left. The thought both excited and terrified you. You didn't know if you were up to task. The love your wife had for you was predicated, in large part, on how much Little Ma liked you, how handsome Little Ma thought you were, how caring, how well-dressed (*What a fine pair of trousers!*), how intelligent, how if Little Ma were younger she would have married you, and on and on…

The next thing you know someone is tweaking your ear. It's Carmen. You'd know her anywhere by that carrot-colored hair. Her face is still cute, but you didn't want to do her in high school so why would you now.

"You're already passed out?" she says. "How late am I!"

You're still a little fuzzy-headed. "Late?"

"The party!"

"You just got here?"

"Oh, come on, get up already," she says, and helps you to your feet. "What's with the Christmas presents, Santa?"

"Julia's gifts to the class masters."

"Should have known," she says, looks through the box and then at you. "So what's with the loaded gun?"

"What?"

"Your pants. I noticed it while you were sleeping." She tussles your hair.

"I wasn't sleeping," you say. "And that's my cell phone. My wife always says I have too many things in my front pants pockets. Says it looks like I have children in there."

"It doesn't look like you have children in there. It looks like a boner in there." She laughs. "I don't care, you can have a boner if you want one."

While you don't really want to have a boner now, you did forget to masturbate this morning. Doesn't matter. You and Carmen used to talk to each other this way in high school all the time. It's not the language of sexual tension; it's the language of two people who enjoy talking mildly dirty with each other. It felt a bit taboo then and still does now. It also feels familiar and comfortable.

"I'm glad you haven't lost your red-headed instincts," you say, and stand up. The two of you start down the hall toward the cafeteria.

"Bit of gray in there, though you can't see it because I pluck and dye out the little bastards."

"Irrelevant," you hear yourself say, one of your favorite expressions from senior year, a kind of shortcut for *What does this have to do with my future, with the meaning of life?*

She laughs. "You still crack me up."

For a second you think she's called you a cracker, which seems odd, accurate, or both—years ago you heard she married a black man. Your high school class was, and you assume still is, 98 percent white. You remember from the website that Carmen and her husband have a daughter—you wonder what she looks like.

"Did your husband come with?"

"Colt is around here somewhere. Can you believe it—he wanted to come. I told him it'd be Dullsville, but he's the class-clown type and thought he'd spice things up."

After Carmen says "clown," you think of Joe Michalszewski and almost tell her about your run-in with him, but instead you just say: "Spice would be good."

You feel bad that there were no black kids in your high school. Or none you knew at least. What kind of person are you anyway? You know you didn't choose to be born where you were born, but you have a choice now. Why don't you know more people who aren't like you?

At the entrance to the cafeteria, you look around. The game tables are more crowded than before. The box is getting heavy. You start to tell this to Carmen, and then she says, "I can't believe you became an English teacher. You hated English."

"Still do."

She thinks you're kidding.

Then she reminds you of the time you were scolded freshman year because you didn't want to read the part of Hamlet.

"I wasn't a good reader then, that's true," you say, "I couldn't pronounce anything and didn't even know what a bodkin was. But I learned to like Hamlet. You can't beat his 'to be or not to be' speech."

"What is it?"

"The speech?"

"No, a bopkin."

"A bodkin is a dagger."

"Why the fancy words—what the fuck happened to *irrelevant*?"

"Guess I changed it into *irreverent*. Hamlet's irreverent. Maybe my saying irrelevant back then to everything I didn't like was just a manifestation of irreverence."

"Maybe," she says. "But I know one thing."

"What's that?"

"You've lost your boner."

You set the box down next to the kitchen door. "Where the hell am I supposed to put this?"

"Oh don't get cranky," she says, "look at me." She points to her chest. "This is all bra, I mean, the bra *is* the boobs."

You try not to think of her boobs; after all you've already ruled out doing her. You change the subject and ask her if she's hungry.

"Thirsty," she says.

"This way," you say, and begin walking, "I used to tend bar at a little hole in the wall down the lane here."

You navigate through what seems like new hordes of people, get a couple of drinks, and finally find a table with two empty chairs. Two nervous-looking women sit there.

"Spouses?" Carmen whispers and sits down.

"My guess."

A couple of large swallows of liquor pass over your lips, hardly touching the inside of your mouth, but they don't make you feel any better.

Carmen starts talking about "class celebrities."

"Who?"

"You know—Tony, Jackie, Scott. I see Tony over there now." She points with her drink. "A whole crowd around him. Like he's going to congratulate you for doing a good job with your life. Please. The guy's a car salesman, and Jackie has varicose veins—I can see them from here. She's a nurse, you think she could get a medical discount."

"You sound like The Professor."

"Who?"

"A friend of mine, a psychologist."

"Honey, you don't need to be a psycho to read these people."

You take another swallow. For a moment you think about the word. Swallowing—isn't it simply another way of marking time?

Carmen says, "You're kind of a celeb yourself, you know."

Through the bottom of your glass you think see Kelly and Jake. But when you lower the glass, it turns out to be another couple with blond hair. "Celeb, how's that?" you say. You put the glass back up to your mouth and look through the bottom again. Down, up, down, up. "I was just a skinny little guy with some promise?"

"Listen," Carmen says, and takes hold of your wrist. "I wasn't going to mention it if you didn't but—"

"My wife."

"I just heard about it—her, I mean, your wife. I'm sorry I didn't know. I mean, Colt and I know about hurricanes in Florida, but we don't have the levees to deal with. What an awful mess. I can't imagine what it must have been like for you."

"What?"

She grips your wrist harder. The two women take sidelong glances at you. "Julia told me everything," Carmen says, "last night at the football game."

"What does Julia know?"

It becomes apparent that, through online exchanges and discussions at the game, a lot of people here know you are a recent widower. You wonder if that's why you've had so many strange or awkward exchanges tonight. Are you the freak, or are they? And now Carmen is telling you about a rumor going around: your wife died in the flood after Hurricane Katrina. One version of the story, she says, even alleges that your wife was trapped in the attic of your home as the waters rose and you couldn't pull her out in time. Carmen wants to know the truth.

"Classic," you say.

"What?" she says.

"Nothing. I was thinking about a piece of music." You would like to set the record straight, if not publicly, then at least for Carmen. But she seems already so invested in the flood story, frankly you don't have the energy to tell her the truth, and even if you correct her, it'll simply add more fuel to the fire. You say you'd rather not talk about it.

"I understand," she says. "But it must be a big job now, taking care of your son alone."

This isn't the Carmen you know and like to be around. This is some kind of false Carmen, who asks the same type of questions everyone else asks. The Carmen you remember would blast through the small talk of tragedy and say exactly what's on her mind even if it's impolite or impolitic. You wonder when she's going to let go of your wrist. Her hand is sweaty.

"People do it all the time," you say.

"I know," she says. "I meant you don't deserve this."

What do you deserve? A medal because you have a sad story. You tell her that, but before she has a chance to respond, you add: "The biggest difference in my life now is the cat. She follows me around the house like a dog. She used to sleep between my wife's legs, now she only wants to sleep right next to my head on the pillow. All night she'll wake me up, nestling and purring. It's fucking annoying. But I don't have the heart to kick her out of the bedroom."

Carmen laughs. "All right," she says, "for the thirtieth reunion, I'll nominate you Most-Likely-To-Be-A-Pussy's-Pussy."

"I'll drink to that," you say, and toast with an empty glass.

Carmen offers to go back to the bar for refills. Before she goes, you ask her if she's seen Kelly Campbell.

"No, why?" she says, and then adds, "what do you want with that cheesy celeb?"

"Just curious," you say. "What about Alex Mueller?"

"I haven't seen him, but someone said he's an actor or something in Germany."

She leaves for the drinks. You smile at the two women who've been listening in. You wait a moment longer, and then you leave. You'll apologize later.

8.

You squeeze in and out and between tables, looking for Alex's face. But then you turn a corner and can't believe your eyes. Brother-in law? No fucking way. You duck behind a pillar. When you take a peek, it's too late—he's spotted you.

He approaches in a fast walk.

"What's up?" you say as casually as possible.

All three hundred pounds of him is huffing and puffing. "Finally," he manages to say, "found you, been looking everywhere."

"I'm right here," you say, "take a breath for god's sake."

"It's Owen."

If your mind doesn't register the words, your body certainly does—chest tightening, sweat flash, heart race. "What?—what—what!—"

"He got a little crushed by some books. One those shelves in the family room—"

"What the fuck do you mean a little? Is he okay—who's taking care of him—where—"

"Hey, slow down," he says, and puts an arm around you, "I'm just screwing with you, bro, Owen's fine."

"What?" you say, pushing his arm away.

He makes a face.

"Owen's fine?"

"He's fine."

"Then what the fuck are you doing here?"

"Take a pill," he says, "I needed a break. Told your sister I was going out for some wine for your dad. That'll buy me an hour or so."

The thought of entertaining him for an hour—or so—

Suddenly a beer appears in front of you, and then: "There you are!" It's the woman Kilroy was ogling—the potato/macaroni salad picker. She's much more attractive close-up. You take the beer from her. "Thanks."

"Who's this?" George says, raising an eyebrow.

"Raina," she says, and holds out her free hand.

"Well, Raina," he says, and shakes her hand, "I'm George—but maybe you should call me Sunshine, as in parting your clouds."

That fucking tears it. Tell George that he's an ass and he's always been an ass. Tell him your sister and niece would be better off without him. Tell him to get lost for good.

"It was a joke, bro," he says, nudging you while looking Raina up and down. "You still pissed from before?"

"What do you *really* want?"

"I told you," he says, "I couldn't take it anymore at your parents' house. Your mom going on and on about office shit. Doctor so-and-so didn't get me the transcriptions in time, CTO conference is a mess, this and that. And the TV blaring...your dad mute in front of it. The place is a nuthouse."

You set down the beer. You've never intentionally hit anyone in your life. Now seems like a fine time. You're about to wind back like you've seen in the movies, when Raina yells "Truce!"

"It's all right," George says. "God love this guy, but I know he's wanted to take a swing at me for a long time."

"How long?" she asks.

"Since Christmas Eve a few years ago," you say, "when we got into an argument about the poor."

"The what?" she says.

"They cheat the system," George says, "and make the rest of us pay for it."

"No, that wasn't the real issue. You were mad because you're still an insurance salesman."

"Software management. Insurance software management."

"Whatever—you had your chance to get out. Go to law school, cooking school or whatever it was you kept moaning about while sitting at home for two years—"

"Taking care of Pearl."

"You had your chance. It's not that hard. I'm doing it."

"Yeah, because—"

"Don't fucking say it."

"Truce," Raina says. "George, it truly was a pleasure to meet you. But this one's mine." She leads you away by the arm.

You mutter *jagoff* under your breath but loud enough for him to hear. Immediately you regret saying it, not because he might hit you or because he doesn't deserve it, but because you're better than this, you like to think of yourself as an even-keeled guy, and you haven't called anyone a jagoff since pick-up soccer games on the middle school playground.

Before you can ask, Raina tells you that Carmen sent her over.

"George's a fucking—"

"Don't bother," she says. "Would you trade places with him?"

"He's my brother-in-law."

"Would you trade places?"

"Hell no."

"Then don't worry about him. Let's go dance."

"I'm not in the boob." You meant to say "mood." Something seems to be wrong with your mouth.

She laughs and it sounds genuine. You can't remember the last time you heard genuine laughter. "I am in the *boob*," she says. She takes a long drink from her beer with one of those mini cocktail straws. Then she turns and starts in the direction of the fieldhouse.

You hesitate. "How do you know Carmen?"

From twenty feet away she beckons you with both arms to follow. "Band," she yells, "trumpet section."

It's a Hawaiian-themed dance, the kind that took place every fall in high school, only no one is wearing Hawaiian shirts and surfer shorts. You wonder what high schools in Hawaii have—Midwestern barnyard dances? Only two couples are on the floor doing a weak waltz to luau music under a silver globe. Raina drags you to floor.

"Who would you trade places with?" you ask.

"It's not a fair question."

"Nothing's fair."

"Of course," she says, "sometimes I'd love to trade places with my sister—she's beautiful, she's got her health and has a ton of money. But I wouldn't want to be her. The things I hold dear are mine, and the things she holds dear are hers. No one wants to trade those."

"That doesn't mean nothing's fair." You realize that didn't make sense. The drinks are piling up in your head. It only takes a couple of them now for you to feel like complete shit the next day.

"Sometimes," you say, "I want to be my father."

"Why do you say it like that—*your father*? You call him father or dad?"

"I don't know," you say, "I guess it's like when I call *my son* my son instead of Owen."

"Why do you want to be your dad?"

"He's made his own world."

"Haven't you?"

"No, I mean in his head—he's made his own world in his head."

You accidentally step on her foot but she doesn't say anything. Your head spins. The dancing, even slowly, doesn't help.

"He's schizophrenic," you say.

"You want to be like him?"

"Don't worry I'm adopted. I'm not nuts. My wife—she was nuts. No, I mean, she was allergic to nuts."

Raina pushes you away.

As with your father's schizophrenia, you seem to be able to reveal your wife's death to total strangers but not to close friends. You recognize this phenomenon in yourself, and you're not altogether happy about it.

"Wife?" she says and walks off toward the doors.

"Dead wife—*was*—aren't you listening?"

She keeps walking. People are watching now. Your first instinct is to get her back. You don't have any other instincts. Like some old boyfriend, you call out, "Rain!" But she has already exited the fieldhouse.

When you finally catch up with her, she says: "It's the old moccasin game—trying to see things from someone else's point of view. But the problem is, when you do that you're not really seeing things from the other person's point of view. It's *you* in those moccasins pretending to be someone else, not actually that someone else. You're still *you*."

"I am, am I?"

"Yes, you are." She's looking at you like she's going to kiss you.

Suddenly you're aware of where you are: The Hall of Fame. You're surrounded by trophy cases and group photographs of championship teams.

"Come here," you say, "I have something to show you."

It doesn't take you long to find the photograph: nine skinny boys in gold and brown running shorts and mesh jerseys. Raina puts her finger against the glass plate over the photo and picks you out instantly—bottom row, kneeling down in the center.

"Jacob's Fighting Eagles: Cross-Country," she says, "Conference Champs 1986."

"I know, pretty lame."

"I already knew about your wife."

"Carmen told you."

She doesn't answer but you know by her eyes. You look back at the photograph and notice your reflection in glass. Raina's reflection is there too, smiling.

"I don't even know you."

"What's there to know?" she says, and places her hands on your shoulders.

You think about it from her perspective: It might be fun and/or perversely erotic to be with a widower. When he puts his mouth on yours, you will feel what she once felt—his soft, firm tongue moving delicately along your lips, his arms grabbing your buttocks and lifting you off the ground, carrying you to the engine hood of some car. Or pushing you up against a brick wall. Wherever you are when it happens, you know he will be rough and hard at first—and then at some point, the love for his wife will release itself and he will collapse into a beautiful weeping mess in your arms. To sleep with so much tragedy— not *le petit mort* but *le grand mort*—how sweet that would be!

If only you could fuck yourself.

"Weird things have happened to me this past year," you say. Her hands fall from your shoulders.

"What do you want to know about me?"

"I don't know," you say, turning around, "something besides you used to play trumpet."

"I was a marine."

"Kilroy mentioned that."

"Who?"

"Nobody."

"What kinds of weird things? Nothing would probably surprise me."

"Could you kill me if you wanted to?"

"What?"

"Being a marine, I mean, you know how to kill people."

"In theory I suppose I do," she says, and takes your hands in hers, "but I never had to kill anyone in the marines. As a cop—"

"You're a cop?"

"Used to be," she says, and squeezes your hands. "You have tension issues."

"They have to do with your holding my hand."

"It's okay, I'm a massage therapist."

"That's a lot of career hopping."

"Actually, I make most of my living as a raw food teacher. My friend David Rolfe got me into it. He's my inspiration. He owns this company called Sunshine Foods in Seattle. Have you heard of it?"

"Sounds new-agey."

"It is, I guess, but it's changed my life. I need about a hundred more years on this earth to accomplish my goals."

"Is this Mr. Rolfe your boyfriend?"

"I wish," she says, pressing her thumbs into your palms, "but he's gay."

"That actually feels good."

"Simple pressure points," she says. "Do you want to sit outside? These fluorescent lights are hurting my eyes."

"Let me say goodbye to the boys."

You turn around and look at the championship photo. You remember most of their names. Andy Walters, Doug Patterson, Scott Pinter, Coach Schwarz. And there in the back row, far right side is the elusive Alex Mueller.

"What's with the stupid grin?" she says.

"Is that a stupid grin?" you say, pointing to yourself in the photo.

"Not there," she says, "there." She points to your mouth.

"I guess I was thinking about the conference meet. It's a boring story."

"I don't believe that," she says, "tell me."

So you tell her all about the varsity cross-country team your junior year. How the team was in fourth place out of five going into the final meet and then slingshotted to tie for conference champs. You even take off your right sock and shoe—because what else is there really to do—to show her your scar. "The guy who came in first place," you say, balancing on one foot, "spiked me right here, on the first step off the line. My shoe was covered in blood by the time I entered the final chute. Didn't matter, though—we were conference champs." It's only after you've finished the story, standing there with your stinking foot, do you realize what a nerd you must look like. But she doesn't make fun.

She says, "Do you want me to take a photo of that photo?"

You consider it a moment. "No, we'll let them stay right here on this wall. They're not going anywhere."

You put your shoe and sock back on. The two of you head for the doors but then someone starts calling for Raina. It's an old friend who begs her to come meet so-and-so and starts pulling her down the hall. Raina looks at you and smiles. "Meet me back here at midnight. I want to show you something." You can't say no—her earnestness is kind of cute. You say sure. She walks away down the hall. For the first time in a long time your only thought is that you'd like to see this person again.

9.

You're back in the cafeteria leaning against a concrete pillar watching the circus. Booze and Vegas. Apparently someone has found the intercom system, and 80's music pumps out of the ceiling speakers. The sound of people talking has risen to meet the need of the music. You look around for a familiar face, though by this point everyone looks familiar. This cast of characters is simply too damn long.

Then you see some of the old clique, plus spouses, gathered around a table. There is Julia, Jewish PTA president, with husband Thad, cell phone store proprietor; Carmen, valedictorian and CPA, with husband Colt, the only black man here; Rick, aerospace engineer, with what looks to be his wife from the way his arm rests on the back of her chair; and, one more couple who you can't place. This could be the last time all of you are together—à la the Last Supper. It won't kill you to make your way over.

There are a few yearbooks sitting on the table but no one is looking at them. Mostly people, in twos, are chatting loudly while downing drinks.

"We didn't have email," someone says, "or cell phones—hell, we didn't even have computers."

There's another side conversation going on about siblings

fighting over the family phone back in high school. It's seems tedious and you think of walking away, but then Carmen sees you and asks how you are.

"Fine," you say, looking for a seat.

"Fine is a grade of sandpaper," she says.

"If you really want to know, I am on the verge of a boner."

Julia laughs, a little too loudly.

This amazes you. The common past of your friends does and doesn't seem to have changed—people look older of course, but their interactions with each other fall into familiar patterns. And so Rick's wife looks uncomfortable not because her skirt suit doesn't fit right but because she doesn't fit into the group. And although you don't have much in common with Rick anymore, you still know how to navigate his personality. Later you will realize this is all bullshit, but for the moment it consoles.

Carmen smiles and nudges you. "It's a boner for Raina, I bet."

Before you can reply, Lane sits down in the remaining empty chair. "Hi," she says and then sees you. "Oh, hi."

You mumble a hello.

"This reunion reminds me of my wedding," Lane says to no one in particular. "I talk to someone for five minutes then someone else for five minutes and on and on, and I never get to eat anything!"

"But plenty of drinks!" says her husband, who has come up behind her and is waving his glass in the air.

"I'm sorry," Thad says, "we met once years ago, but I can't remember your name."

Lane's husband says "J" something and slurs the rest.

"JP?"

"J...D."

"Right, JD...JD..."

"You have a law degree?" Colt interrupts, "I need a lawyer."

Julia changes the subject: "Can you believe this night? Everybody looks so good."

"Actually," Carmen says, "I threw up a little when I heard you were rounding up all the burnouts, preppies, and break dancers for this."

"Oh come on," Lane says, "you love it."

"I don't," Carmen says, "but I do love seeing all of you again."

"That's better," Julia says.

JD turns to you, "I hear you're an adjudicator."

"I could use a lawyer," Colt says.

"Is that what an adjudicator is?" Lane asks.

"I meant educator," JD says.

"You're drunk," Lane says.

"You wish," JD says.

You sense an ongoing argument. The husband who always has to be right and the wife who always has to point out he's not. You imagine later, at her parents' house, she'll go to bed in a funk and he'll go downstairs and lie on the living room couch, lacking the energy to pour himself a drink from the bar-on-wheels across the room or to stop the dog from chewing on his dress shoes.

"What's this lawyer stuff?" Carmen says to her husband.

"These red-necks—not you folks," Colt says, and waves his hand. "Those people out there. Not one of them would talk politics with me. I wanna sue."

You can't tell whether Colt is drunk, like everyone else, or just combative by nature.

JD turns to you: "*Ed-u-ca-tor*...tell us more."

"He teaches high school online," Carmen says.

"McDonald Virtual High School," you say, "for home schooled kids, returning students, prisoners."

"Virtual high," Julia says, "that's cute."

"Like fast food?" JD says.

Rick's wife says, "I've heard about that school. It was on NPR, right?"

"Last year."

"I always meant to look it up," she says. "Seems like an idea that's long overdue. I bet you don't have any of these high school cliques to deal with."

"It's not right for every kid, but for some...."

"Do you like it?"

"I think it sounds weird," Thad says. You didn't think he was even listening. "No disrespect, I mean, high school is where you find yourself. Not online."

"Really?" Colt says, "high school was a blur to me—I found myself in college."

"Damn," Lane says, "you already found yourself? I'm still looking!"

There is awkward laughter.

For a moment you consider saying *I never want to find myself* or *I don't like who I've found.*

You lose track of the conversation until there is a burst of laughter, and it seems in response to something but you're not sure what. You suspect that everyone is making fun of your job—or you—and that they never really liked you. There is no doubt that at eighteen you were a smartass who wasn't very smart and a pain in the ass who didn't know much about pain.

"I'll talk politics with you," Rick says to Colt.

Rick's wife squeezes his arm.

"Colt was screwing with you," Carmen says to Rick. "It's part of his wily charm."

Rick looks deflated.

"I curry favor with no man," you say. It's a bad attempt at

humor. At the least you expect Carmen to save you. But no one says anything.

"I like politics," Lane says, "especially Civil War reenactments."

At this, separate conversations break out. Carmen leans over to you and whispers, "I know she was my friend, but Lane's as stupid as ever. I can't believe she replicated herself four times. How the fuck did you date her, and why the fuck did I let you?"

"I may have fucking dated her, but I never fucked her on a date."

"Nice one," she says.

"Glad to see you've not given up on swearing," you say. "I'd thought that after all these years, maybe you'd outgrown it."

"Outgrown? You kidding—cussing keeps me honest. People are hypocrites who don't cuss. Everybody shits, you know."

"Sure, I know, my son calls it *poofs*."

"Nice."

"When he has to fart, he says *cheeeesy*."

"Clever boy."

"I'd like to take the credit," you say, "but one of his little friends taught him that." You sense you're being dull. Colt is talking with Rick now. "I forgot to ask, what does Colt do?"

"Small business owner," Carmen says. "He has—"

"No," Colt interjects, "*we* have a barbeque restaurant. *Together*, Red, that's the deal."

"He runs the show," Carmen says. "I just do the books once a month."

Colt goes back to his discussion with Rick. They're on to foreign policy and war can't be too far behind.

Julia lifts Lane's hand and admires her wedding ring. "That's gorgeous."

"JD picked the stone himself," Lane says, finishing her drink. The class ring you bought junior year immediately comes to mind. You bought it for $150, earned by mowing neighbors' lawns, so that Lane could wrap purple yarn around the band and wear it on her ring finger.

"Thad picked out my ring, too," Julia says, displaying her hand.

"That's very nice," Lane says. "But I meant JD went out and smashed it out of a rock. How romantic is that?"

JD blushes.

"He didn't have any money, but he had a friend who knew where to look for sapphires."

"This was in Australia," JD adds.

Lane continues, "He had the stone in hand when he proposed to me. Said someday when he got the money, he'd have it cut and mounted on a ring. It took him until our fifth anniversary, but he did it."

"That's not even the good part of the story," JD says. "Tell them about your father."

"Oh yes," she says. "Dad didn't like JD, you know, that he didn't have any money. But Mom liked him right away."

"The funny part, come on."

"I'm getting there, sweetheart," she says. "So the first time JD met my parents, Dad sat him down in the living room and said, 'Son, I suppose this is going to happen but before it does I have one question I want an honest answer to—is there any history of mental illness in your family?'"

JD laughs. "He was so serious about it."

"Of course he was," she says.

"And of course I had to lie," JD says. "My Uncle Bill was totally nuts."

"I don't get it," Thad says to JD, "you're Australian?"

"Oh no," Lane says, "he went there for junior year abroad.

It was great for him, but hard on me."

The professional photographer is suddenly at your elbow. "Sir, could you please move that way," he says to you, "there, there." You do as you're told and get uncomfortably close to JD. The photographer wants you to put your arm around him. You obey. The mix of JD's breath and Lane's perfume—no longer the Estee Lauder White Linen she wore in high school—is bizarrely alluring. Just as you detect a rise in your pants, the photographic moment is over. JD excuses himself to the men's room, and the women begin talking among themselves.

In the distance, you observe two men embracing while another man takes their picture. If you've had any grand epiphanies since last year, it is that proximity is the best criterion for friendship. After college, people meet new friends only at work or through their children's friends. Your work is virtual; your child is not yet two. Because it only depresses you, you do not ask yourself very often who your best friend is. You've had them over the years, in this or that place you've lived, but who would you call your best friend now? After your dead wife is ruled out, the next candidate is The Professor. But he can be such an ass, and you cannot have an ass as a best friend. It's not uncommon or even sad not to have a best friend; your father doesn't have any friends at all, except your mother, and your mother's best friend was her mother, until she died ten years ago and so now your mother's best friend is your father. No, it's not sad, it simply is.

You take the last mouthful of bourbon and hold it between teeth and gums, trying to balance it there as if in the liminal state between waking and sleeping where, incidentally, your best ideas come. This time, however, it feels overly stylized and you haven't had a good idea in ages. You realize this is the longest you've sat down the entire night. The voices around you are pinballing. The room has become very small. Your breath feels stuck inside your chest.

You try to tune in one of the conversations. Julia and Carmen are reminiscing about the time you yakked in the back of Julia's orange Vega, after lying about drinking beforehand. Lane and JD are standing now and seem to be arguing about whether he's going outside to smoke a cigar. The unknown couple is talking about some high school party, where somebody drank a cup of chewing tobacco on a dare. "Gross!" someone says passing by. From an adjacent table you hear: "The Gluck twins—they were so tight, I thought they'd marry each other." The conversations run too fast around you to catch up with any of them. You look over at the gaming tables, arms moving, legs swaying, little architectures of people.

Rick taps your shoulder, "Don't you live in New Orleans?"

Haven't we covered this already? you think.

He starts talking about the levees and the wetlands or something. You find it hard to concentrate on his words. Then Thad interjects something about his one visit to the city and seeing flying geckos. You consider correcting Mr. Know It All, but there's no point in being right if it'll upset him; his upset will become your upset. You make a lot of *uh-huh* sounds.

From behind you a squeaky voice says, "Oh, he was one of those people who thought he was destined for greater things. I bet he's a community college professor and happily divorced."

You turn suddenly and say, "High school and I'm not divorced." But apparently they aren't talking about you, and they don't even notice you've said anything.

"My ex-husband was a first-class tool," a woman says. "Thank god I never have to see the bastard again."

"I envy your divorce," another woman says. "My ex was screwing someone at work. We split up but I still have to see him because of Louis, our son."

"I'm just so busy," the first woman says, "between work, the kids' activities, and seeing family, there's no time for much else."

"What else is there?"

"Hobbies?"

"We took ballroom dance lessons years ago. That was before the kids."

"My husband insisted I take watercolor painting last spring."

"My husband always says his hobby is sex. But he never gets to do it. I tell him, I'm not a hobby. He says, 'You're my hobby horse.'"

The women laugh hysterically.

Back at your table the conversation has turned to raising kids. You've already concluded that your classmates are not as divided along old high school lines as much as they are along a new demarcation: those who have children and those who don't. Parents talk easily with each other about sleep deprivation, potty training, charter schools, etc. (Except for parents whose teenagers are about to graduate high school; they are part of their own new clique and mostly still live in town.)

You go in and out of paying attention until Rick's wife says, "I don't think I've ever seen a child ride a bicycle without his helmet?"

"Listen, honey," Thad leans over to Rick's wife, "I've never bought one of the damn things for our kids. If I didn't need one as a kid, they don't now."

"Oh, Thad's joking with you," Julia says, "of course our sons wears helmets."

"What the hell are you talking about—I never bought any, waste of money."

Julia gives Thad a stern look, but he shakes it off, literally, and spills some of his beer onto the table. "Christ!" he says and swats at it with a dirty napkin.

You'd like to tell the story about a friend of yours who split his head open after being sideswiped by a truck and underwent brain surgery, leaving him with no sense of smell or taste. But by the time you're ready to speak up, the topic has changed to biting.

"I'd just bite him back," Thad says. He's giving advice to Lane and JD, whose three-year-old son likes to bite his classmates and, occasionally, mommy and daddy.

Rick says, "That doesn't sound very prudent."

"Prudent—I didn't say it was, but it'll work!"

There's some talk of baby gadgets, videos vs. books, etc. You feel like you should add something useful. "I use baby wipes for everything."

"Like what?"

"Hand sanitizers—and oh, to clean the windshield, the shower, the toilet. Sometimes Owen and I get down on the floor and start washing it with wipes. He especially likes—"

"You can't use baby wipes for the shower," Lane says.

"Why not?" Carmen says.

"It's not—I don't know—it's not sanitary."

Everyone laughs and you try to follow, but you're not sure whether they're laughing at Lane or at you.

Then Julia asks Colt, "I heard you got Carmen to stop swearing in front of the kids. What's the trick?"

"Money jar," Colt says. "She had to put twenty bucks into it every time she said shit, fuck, or even fart."

"That worked?" you ask.

"No, but I made a few hundred bucks and bought a new TV with it!"

"He came up with something better," Carmen says, "Sex

coupons. Gave me some cunnilingus coupons and some two-for-ones, which meant I got an extra orgasm for every one he had."

"I don't get it," Julia says.

"He gave me the coupons and then each time I'd cuss in front of the kids, he'd take one back. I didn't get laid for three weeks."

"And that did it," Colt says.

"Figured actual fucking was better than talking about it," Carmen says and gives Colt a big kiss on the cheek.

The women begin regaling about the miracle of childbirth and the men appear bored. You look at your watch. It's only a quarter to eleven. Colt, Rick, and Thad form a posse to hunt down drinks. JD is too smashed to stop leaning into his wife. You join the posse.

The four of you wait in a long line.

"Men don't like children," Rick says.

"What do you mean, of course they—we—do," Colt says.

"No," Thad says, "I think Rick may have a point."

"I think I always knew it, you know, but it hit me hard last year. I left our son at the grocery store."

"What?"

"It was an accident. I had a lot on my mind about work and the lab, and I just forgot about him—was already in the car pulling out of the parking lot."

"Jesus," Thad says, "how'd you ever live that one down."

"You think I told her? Anyway, it was a sign that part of me wanted to leave the little guy there. Don't get me wrong, I love our son but...."

"He's sometimes hard to like," Thad says.

"Something like that," Rick says. "He's my stepson anyway."

Your feet start to hurt, damn new shoes. You look around

but there's not a free chair. Why won't this line move?

"I love *and* like my kids," Colt says.

"Regular Mr. Mom," Thad says.

"No, not at all," Colt says, "I work forty, hell, fifty hours a week *and* help with the kids."

"You're atypical anyway," Thad says.

"What?"

"Come on, look around...." Thad says.

There's a sudden kink in the line and everyone lunges forward.

Thad doesn't finish his sentence, but you guess he meant that Colt is the only black guy here.

"Jockitch," Rick says and pats you, not unlike a pet, on the shoulder, "you're pretty quiet over there."

Or is it that Colt's married to the foul-mouthed valedictorian? Or that he owns his own business?

Rick seems to be waiting for an answer from you.

"I'm thinking you're rowing a sinking canoe."

They all look at you in confusion, and there's a long pause until Thad says, "Look, my buzz is wearing off and I'm tired of waiting. I've got a few bottles of wine in the car."

Colt stays in line. Rick and Thad head for the doors. You don't really want to stay or go. Then you see Kelly—you think—but she's not with her blond husband, she's with some dark-haired guy. Your eyes hurt, maybe it's not her. In any event, you're too tired to make another trip to the parking lot.

You're staring at the long, wavy hair of the woman in front of you in line. It's so damn similar to your wife's. You think about running your hands in and out of it. You think about your wife's head, how she loved you to massage it—how a massage was almost the only way you could get her to have sex with you after the baby.

You hear yourself say, "Can I ask you a personal question?"

"All right," Colt says.

"What are your thoughts about married sex?"

"You kill me," he says. "Carmen was right when she said you were full of random shit."

"Oh."

"That's a compliment," he says. "But don't tell me that now you're gay?"

"No, I didn't mean sex with me."

He laughs. "I mean, I know you aren't gay—or weren't—Carmen told me about that time you two hooked up, too."

While patently untrue, you are flattered that Carmen lied. "I'm wondering…" you say, but then can't seem to formulate what it is you want to say.

"Aren't you married?"

Here we go again. You lift your left hand. "I removed the band six months ago. After the dishes met the pavement."

"What?"

"Never mind."

"All I know," he says, "is that I knew the sex would drop off after getting married, but I didn't think it'd totally tank."

You remember what The Professor once said about his ex-wife, *I don't think she'd even known what to do with her genitalia if I hadn't shown her.*

"I guess," Colt says, "I've learned to work on it."

"Sex?"

"Marriage."

The line lurches forward again.

"It's like owning a home," he says, "as soon as you get one thing fixed something else falls apart."

You attempt a joke: "And you have to do your own maintenance."

"Right," he says, "you definitely shouldn't hire somebody else to do it."

You consider this and begin calculating the sum of all the times you were a jerk to your wife and the sum of all the times she was a jerk to you—would they cancel each other out? And if so would that make it okay? Those times when she would say *Do you always have to be on the computer? Come to bed.* You'd remind her that it was your job to be on the computer, even if you were looking at internet porn because she was too tired to put out. That expression has never made sense to you since it's actually something she has to put in, or perhaps put between—which would have made you come to bed. You're not a sex maniac, after all, like you've heard her grandfather was: for thirty-seven years, he demanded it from her grandmother every day, sometimes twice a day, even after diabetes took both of her legs below the knee. Another line from The Professor comes to mind: *You have to love like an ass before your wife will fuck you in it.*

For some reason, people are getting out of line and you move quickly forward. Colt puts in the drink order.

By the time you return to the table, only Carmen and Rick and his wife remain. You still haven't caught her name, and it's too late now.

"The auction is about to start," Carmen says.

"Who are they auctioning off?" Colt says.

Rick doesn't flinch this time.

"I'm messing with you," Colt says, and moves to backslap Rick and then doesn't.

Rick turns to you, "Coming?"

The commons is filled with classmates, their spouses, and a handful of the parent volunteers. Your clique begins moving toward the front. On the way you pass by Julia's parents standing off to one side, holding hands. They smile and wave at you. At least maybe that worked out. Julia stands behind a podium. She's making her thank-yous to the organizers, parents, etc.

You look around at all the people. You're tired of thinking about them, wondering, pontificating in your head about all the things you can't know and will never know. Except—it hits you—Alex Mueller. Did he ever show? You scan the crowd once more.

"…but it's not over yet, folks," Julia says. "Now it's time for the goodies!"

You're about as interested in auctions as you are in baseball games. Both raise a lot of expectations they can't keep.

As Julia lists off the items to be auctioned, which are lined up on a small stage, Jackie points to each of them like a game show hostess. The big-ticket item is the trip to Suriname, which is apparently an eco-vacation.

"Suriname," Lane says. "Where the hell is that? Why didn't they pick something normal like Disney World or Cancun?"

"There's no *eco* at Disney," Carmen says. "Disney's the opposite of eco."

"We've been to Epcot five times," Lane says.

"That's so unrealistic," Carmen says.

"Tell her, JD, we've been there five times."

"No, Epcot is unrealistic," Carmen says.

"Well, I guess," Lane laughs. "But it makes the kids happy."

"You're kids maybe," Carmen says.

You wait for Lane's husband to swoop in—change the subject, slap Carmen, or punch you because you're standing next to her. A bloody nose might liven this party up. Where is that photographer when you need him? An action shot would be perfect for the post-reunion, follow-up email that will likely be sent out.

But nothing happens.

The auction begins, complete with speed-talking auctioneer. The first item is a framed photo of the senior class. Oh Lord. You're feeling light-headed again. Probably low-blood sugar. You ask but no one else is hungry. The bidding on the photo is already up to $50 in fake money.

The floor is packed so you have to find an alternate route to the food table. You wander into a corner by mistake. There are photos of five classmates posted on a pegboard. It looks like one of those science project stands you made in middle school. Underneath each of their names are dates of birth and death. You've stumbled on the "Memorial Corner." People have written little tributes and anecdotes about each of the dead. Dora of the Hodgkins' Disease was the first to go at nineteen. The latest death was only two months ago, breast cancer. The only deceased male is a guy you used to feel sorry for (and avoid) because he was poor and smelled. If he were here now, you know you wouldn't want to talk to him. It's too bad you can't talk to the dead; they would probably be less repetitive than the living. Julia should have had larger nametags that included occupation, martial status, and numbers of kids. That could have eliminated a lot of wasteful banter.

"Nice graveyard," you hear from behind.

It's Kilroy.

"Uh-huh."

"I wonder what she looks like now," he says and points to Dora's photo.

"Skeletal and mealy."

"No, I mean if she had lived and were here now."

"Couldn't guess."

He bends over to get a closer look at the photos. After a moment where he seems to be trying to look up the skirt of the woman who died of breast cancer, he leans back and says, "Dude, what's with the auction right on top of the graveyard?"

"Couldn't guess." You kind of appreciate the juxtaposition and try to recall a homily to fit the occasion. But your attention is taken by Kilroy's sway, back and forth, which is quite exquisite as his drink splashes around in his glass without spilling over the sides.

"I heard about this woman in Des Moines," he says, "she won a $10,000 funeral at a minor league baseball game."

"Right then and there," Carmen says, "they buried her in the outfield, did they?" She must have followed you.

Kilroy laughs the laugh of a man who's being made fun of. You feel sorry for him. Or maybe it's residual pity for the dead smelly guy. You can't take your eyes off of Kilroy's glass which is still pitching back and forth.

"This guy is loaded," Carmen says.

"This guy is Kilroy," Kilroy says.

"This is Carmen," you say to him.

"At your service, madame." He mock kisses her hand.

"Who are you with?"

"I'm with my wife."

"Who's she?"

"She's my wife."

"No, I mean, what's her name," Carmen says. "You're not a classmate, are you?"

"I am," he says, lifting his glass to his face. "Don't you recognize me?"

She takes in his face for a moment. "Nope."

He points to you, "I've been following this guy around all night, wondering when he'd remember."

It hits you—did Kilroy send the mysterious email threatening to beat your face in? You're hesitant, but you say, "Remember what?"

"Senior year, the last week of school. At the awards assembly in the gym." Kilroy says it as if he's been practicing. "I was playing the snare drum, doing this awesome solo. And you fucking de-pants me in front of everybody."

You try to process what he's talking about, but nothing is coming up.

"*Everybody*," he says.

"I remember that," Carmen says with a laugh. "I got out of playing in band because I had to give a speech. It was like my dress rehearsal for graduation day. I watched the spectacle from the front. You stood there forever banging away at that drum, until Mrs. Brown threw something around you, a coat or something—she didn't dare pull your pants back up."

You're having a hard time recalling any of this, but you apologize anyway.

"No, no," Kilroy says, "I'm *glad* you did it. That's my point. It was a defining moment for me."

You try not to picture him standing in his underwear.

"By the time I realized my pants were down it was too late. I just powered through the solo. I'd been made fun of so many times before that—I don't know—something in me just kept going."

"I remember that too," Carmen says, "after a while the whole gym cheered you on. It was amazing."

"The next day," Kilroy says, "I drove into Chicago and signed up to be a seaman. I didn't think I had the balls to do it before that."

You don't know what to say. They both must be completely ploughed.

"I thought you'd remember," he says. His face looks sad or tired, you can't tell which. He takes a sip of his drink right before it looks like it'll splash him in the face.

"I remember now," you say. "It was funny, wasn't it."

"It was hysterical," Carmen says.

Kilroy raises his glass to your face. "I just wanted to say thanks," he says. "Here's to old Jockitch."

You raise an imaginary glass to his.

"I really should get back to my wife," he says. "She's circling around here somewhere. If you want, we're meeting a couple of friends later at the IHOP down on Randall Road."

"Thanks," you say, "I'll try to make it."

Kilroy raises his glass once more to you and Carmen and then he disappears into the crowd.

As soon as he's gone, Carmen turns to you. "It wasn't you, of course."

"What?"

"It was Rick who de-pantsed him. Rick and that fat guy who played tuba."

"Honestly," you say, "I don't think I was even there."

"You didn't want to burst his bubble, did you?"

"I guess not."

"But you have no intention of seeing him later, do you?"

"No."

The only items left on the food table are a few stranded carrot and celery sticks and wilted egg salad finger sandwiches. You grab the sandwiches and shove them in your mouth.

"You must be desperate," Carmen says, "I mean for food."

"Drinks?" you say, egg salad bits flying.

When you get back to the auction, you find that Rick has won a stuffed animal, the kind one finds at a theme park. It's an eagle, the school's mascot. He says he knows it's dumb but he promised to bring home something for their son.

"I think I need a couple of those goldfish," Carmen says, pointing to the next item up for bid. "I'm going to dare my husband to eat one live."

"Where is he anyway?" you ask.

"He went back to the hotel already, claiming jet leg."

"Jet *lag?*"

"Yeah, didn't I say that?"

"You said...oh never mind."

The bidding starts at a dollar but soon it's twenty and then jumps to fifty.

"For fucking fish!" Carmen says. "I don't care if it is fake money. I'm not paying that."

"You sound like my mother," you say.

"Bite your tongue, Jockitch."

"Bitten," you say, which is difficult to say when actually biting your tongue.

For the next fifteen minutes people around you bid and jump up and down when they've won something. Lane wins a matching scarf and winter hat. Thad wins a hibachi grill. Rick wins a Rubik's Cube. Carmen ends up with a couple of gift certificates: "I'll use them for Christmas presents."

You almost tell her that's what your mother would do.

You're happy for your old friends, who seem to take some delight in their prizes. None of it seems worth hauling back home until the 60" widescreen plasma TV comes up for bid. The auctioneer, a man wearing jeans and regulation plaid flannel, begins to describe the TV's features. And you begin to imagine Owen and yourself watching the TV while lying in bed, your arm nestled around him. It's Saturday afternoon, college football on five different channels. A bowl of popcorn between you—when he's older, of course, and can eat popcorn. For now, he has a cookie and you have a beer. No. A six-pack, a box of cookies. When there's an amazing catch, you show Owen how to use the built-in playback. *What a beautiful fucking TV.* The two of you could watch all the college bowl games on it, then the NFL playoffs and Super Bowl. Suddenly you must have the TV. This is what you came here for. This is tangible. And not only is it fair for you to get the TV, it's fucking due you.

The bidding starts at $100. You have a few hundred left in your envelope. No one else seems to have any money left except Rick.

"Could I have it?" you say.

"No," he says.

"Give it to him," Carmen says.

Rick hands you $400.

The bidding is up to $500 already. You raise your hand, "Six-hundred."

There are three or four other bidders in the crowd. Soon the bidding it up to eight-hundred. This thing is yours. *Due me, due me, due me*, you mumble, and then realize Carmen is staring at you. She smiles. You bid all you have, but then someone quickly bids a thousand. Carmen hands you another three-hundred she's managed to solicit from others—*It's for his grandmother in home hospice*—and suddenly people you don't even know are coughing up fake bills, someone even slips in a real twenty. At two thousand, which you don't even have yet, it's between you and someone you can't exactly see on the other side of the commons.

The people standing or sitting near you are cheering you

on; even Lane and JD are chanting "Jock-itch! Jock-itch! Jock-itch!" The trickle of money, though, has run dry. Your enthusiasm wanes.

"Who the hell is that bidding against you?" Thad says.

"It's that woman who won the lottery," says Rick's wife.

"What an assholette," Carmen says. "Doesn't she have enough real fucking money?"

"It's probably a golden ball and chain," says Rick's wife. "I kind of feel sorry for her—have you seen her dumpy boyfriend?"

Then you remember the silver money clip that Joe gave you. You dig inside your pockets but can't feel it. You get down on your knees and empty everything onto the floor—wallet, keys, phone, change, receipts. No clip.

You're still looking between people's legs when Carmen lays a hand on your shoulder. "It's over."

She helps you gather your things. I'm sorry," she says, "at least Miss Moneybags didn't win."

"Who did?"

"I don't know, somebody slipped in at the last-minute."

"Here you go," Thad says, and hands you a light beer. "Forget about the TV. Who has the room for it anyway? Let's get you that vacation."

"I don't want the vacation."

"You've probably got enough money now," Carmen says.

"But it's Suriname," Lane says.

"Shut the fuck up," Carmen says.

"It's okay," you say, "Lane's right. I don't want to go to Suriname."

You feel like these people are bogging you down with their pity. You give your small fortune of fake money to Carmen and excuse yourself to the men's room.

It's empty, thank god. But where are the urinals?

Jesus, you're in the ladies' room.

Backing out you bump into a woman and mumble an apology.

In the men's room, you pick the second farthest urinal and set the beer precariously on top. Unzip. Nothing's changed in here—should it have? It's a john. You're there a while trying to piss. You look around and see the back of yourself in the mirror. No bald spot yet. It's odd to see the back of your own head. Everyone must see it a lot, that wave in your hair you're almost never aware of. As your bladder finally releases, you study yourself in the mirror. This is you, this is your life. A man alone in a toilet, half-drunk, thinking he is alone in a toilet, half drunk.

Suddenly your olfactory sense takes a hit—the strong scent of cheap cologne. Brut, Polo, Old Spice? Then a thought— isn't all cologne cheap by definition? You hear a stall door lock shut.

You're still pissing, one of those long pisses you didn't really know was in there until it began. Your mind wanders back to the girl who had Hodgkins' Disease. You liked Dora when she was in elementary and middle school—not particularly cute but a smart, sweet girl. The truth is, however, you didn't like the person Dora became by the end of high school. She got in with the popular crowd and started to cop an attitude. It could have been a reaction to her slowly dying, using the attention of cancer to get in as much life as possible. Who could blame her for that? Sometimes you do. She died the year after graduation and now it is nineteen years later: she would have been thirty-eight like everyone else. There is only one question left to answer: What are you supposed to do with all of these thoughts of her? There's no proper category to stuff them into, no hole to flush them down, no place to let them go. She's still with you, and it is as unremarkable as it is uncomfortable.

The stall door opens and it's Dick Ambrosio. He liked to be called Dick because he had a big one—thirteen inches apparently, though you never saw the photo his girlfriend sent around school. Without washing his hands, he leaves. You've missed your chance again.

10.

It's after midnight. The auction is in its last throes. You circumvent the crowd and turn down a hallway. You're late. It's empty except for two men walking toward you at a brisk pace. They are a regular Abbott and Costello—one fat, one skinny. Fatty has his arm around Skinny. What strikes you is that in high school you don't remember either one of them having anything to do with the other. Fatty was the dumb football type and Skinny was a math geek. Fatty's arm looks heavy on Skinny's shoulder. As you pass, Skinny says to Fatty: "No, man, I'm not your Asian." This seems emblematic of something about the reunion at large, but you're not sure what.

You turn the corner and walk through the Hall of Fame to the set of double-doors. There's no sign of Raina. Maybe you missed her. Maybe she was playing with you.

Your mouth tastes a little funny. You wonder if your breath stinks. You feel like you've made an ass of yourself the entire evening. As soon as you decide to call it a night, she arrives.

"You're standing in the same spot you were when I left. Looks like you've been standing here the whole time."

"Something like that," you say.

"I didn't know if you'd come."

"You said you wanted to show me something?"

"I hope I do," she says, "if it's still there."

"What's still where?"

She puts her index finger to her lips as if she's shushing you but doesn't make the shush. She takes your hand and leads you back down the Hall of Fame and then pushes a door that opens onto a stairwell. You remember this stairwell—you and Lane used to make-out between classes under it. Face all flushed and lips bitten, you'd amble to trig or econ or wherever thinking only about the next meeting under the stairwell.

Raina starts climbing the stairs.

"Where are we doing?"

"What, you afraid of the dark?"

"Maybe."

She takes out her cell phone and opens it. A small, dim circle illuminates a few feet in front of you. She starts taking the stairs two at a time. You lag behind, feeling your way. She's probably half a flight ahead.

"I want to see if it's still there," she says. Her voice sounds far away and close-up at the same time.

"What's still where?"

"My time capsule. You're kind of slow."

"What?"

"The last week of school I put it up there, hurry."

"What's the hurry, it's not going anywhere if it's still— where is it?"

"The roof."

This woman is either perfect for you or too much too handle. You can't decide which. But she is right here, right now, and like listening to a pop song again and again, until either you fall asleep or your ears bleed out, she might be exactly what you need.

On a landing you accidentally bump into her. "I'm sorry."

"I'm not," she says.

"What makes you think the roof is going to be open?"

"I still have the key the janitor gave me."

"You're something else," you say.

"Come on," she says, squeezing your hand, "run away with me."

"Shouldn't we get to the top first?"

On the roof Raina immediately heads for a vent or something vent-like and begins rummaging around. The ground is sticky and gravelly, like sand over lotioned skin, and it's darker than you thought it would be. No flood lights, only a low hanging moon. There isn't much to see from over the edges of the building, just the parking lot on one end, the football field and track behind the school, and subdivisions in the distance.

You make your way over to her in the diffuse light.

"It's not here," she says.

"Are you sure?"

She lowers her head. "Maybe I dreamed it."

"You dreamed hiding a time capsule?"

"I don't know, it was a long time ago." She seems disappointed but doesn't want to let on.

"Let's look again."

"No," she says, "let's run away instead."

"I thought you were speaking metaphorically."

"No, I mean it—let's run away."

"From what?"

"Not from *anything*," she says, "but to *something*."

"Something what?"

"Different."

"I'm already different."

"Are you intentionally being difficult?" she says, and puts

her hands around your waist. Half an hour ago this is where you'd hoped things would go, but now you're not sure.

"I don't even know you."

"You already said that once tonight."

"Touché."

"All right," she says, and guides your hips to sit down with her. "If it's not already clear, this is what you need to know about me: I want you to stick it in me. And we don't have to be friends afterward."

"I know," you say, "I already vowed to myself an hour ago that I couldn't make any new friends until one of my old friends dies."

She laughs and then leans back on her arms. "Sometimes," she says, "I think there's only a handful of different types of people in the world. When I was stationed in Germany, I met a guy from Spain whose personality, his way of acting, his mannerisms were exactly like my boyfriend's in college. The language and culture may have been different but the person was the same. Then it happened again with a friend's girlfriend and my sister. It wasn't simply similar traits—hair color, being overly neat, favorite movies—but gestures, ways they tilted their heads when they were thinking hard. Then I began to see these parallels between people even when I wasn't even looking for them. Sometimes I do think that it's only *me*. That I'm making these connections because of who I am, my mind matching them up, not because of how they really are. It doesn't matter either way, I guess, but it still haunts me that almost everyone reminds me of someone else."

You resist asking her the obvious question: *Who do I remind you of?*

"Now will you fuck me," she says, stretching her arms over her head.

Part of you wants to, part of you doesn't.

"Don't worry," she says, "I can't have kids." She puts your hand on her abdomen. "Bad parts."

Then she puts her hand on your thigh. You remove your hand from her abdomen and put it on her breast slowly, poking it in a deliberate, melodramatic way. Surely this will defuse sexual tension. You even let out a small laugh.

But she's not laughing. She already has her eyes closed and looks as though she's on the beach, waiting for the sunlight to warm her face in a glow. Her mouth is slightly open and it doesn't look innocent, it looks French. Would kissing her constitute betrayal?

Before you can consider this any further, she has pulled you to her and her lips are against your neck right below your left ear. There is a small rise and then a full erection. This shouldn't be happening. It's fine to get a hard-on for a woman now and then, but to press up against one of their midriffs.... You try to think of your wife. What if she were doing this to some guy at her reunion? Raina's now on to your other ear, the tip of her tongue tracing the outside. You've never liked ear-probing much—it's been years since anyone's tried—but now it's sending hot chills to your pith.

You do and do not want to press your lips hard against her.

Then it simply happens and continues to happen for a few minutes, in a kind of tug-of-war, push and pull, until finally she's at arm's length.

"Am I the first woman you've kissed since...." You wait for her to finish the sentence but she can't or won't.

"No," you say, "that would be my mother-in-law."

"Not on the cheek, I mean."

"I mean, not on the cheek."

She wants the full story. "I would prefer not to," you say.

You think about putting your hands around her face, and then think better of it. You take turns staring at the ground and the sky.

Suddenly she stands and quotes a poem to you, one of her favorites she says:

> Mind led body
> to the edge of the precipice.
> They stared in desire
> at the naked abyss.
> If you love me, said mind,
> take that step into silence.
> If you love me, said body,
> turn and exist.

You think of Beckett's *I can't go on. I'll go on.*

"Is that," you say, "supposed to remind you not to jump off a cliff?"

"No," she says, "it's supposed to remind me I have a body."

"How can you forget about it?"

"No, how can *you* forget about it," she says. You look at her silhouetted against the sky. It's not her body that attracts you (you've seen better) so much as her voice. In the near-dark, the throaty rasp of it is more pronounced, and the way she overemphasizes the sounds of letters, especially b's and p's, is alluring. She says, "Kiss me again or I'll jump."

"Excuse me?"

She walks over to the edge of the building. "Come here and put one on me."

You feel your breath quicken and your hands sweat. It's the same response you have when you're watching your son as he navigates sharp corners and then nails one with his temple; you see the event before it happens, before your arm can push a chair out of the way or your hand can cover up a dangerous object.

"I don't think so," you say. "Afraid of heights."

"Have it your way."

Before you can respond, she turns around and jumps.

You get to your feet and race to the edge. You expect the worst. You have to. At first you can't see exactly what's happened—your glasses have come off making everything a cloudy blur—and then you see what looks like a hand waving at you. "Come on down!"

She's only jumped down to the roof of the floor below. You yell: "This a game to you?"

"Price is right—free!—come on get me!"

You jump down but she runs. By the time you catch her you've broken a sweat, not out of exertion but nerves, and when you grab her, your face adheres against hers. Your shirt comes off, her skirted is hiked, her tongue is inside your mouth, it is twisting you inside out, her tights are gone, thrown off the building you hope, your pants are around your knees, her knees are around your waist, the middle finger of your right hand is underneath her and suddenly touches the spot between her vagina and anus, both are wet, she makes a sweet sound, you try to make none, your left arm balancing her on top, you throw her into the air, when she comes down, her hands are clenched around your neck and then are pulling your hair, your cock gets sucked up into her and, in a moment of clear consciousness, you wonder if you'll ever get yourself out. You open your eyes for a second—her eyes are squeezed tight, her mouth wide open. Who does she think is fucking her? Who is this fucking her?

It lasts about five minutes.

When you try to lift her off, you both collapse on the ground.

It feels good to lie there with a stranger on top of you. You try not to hold her too tightly. Soon you sense she is sleeping or on the threshold of sleep. You imagine her tomorrow morning— she'll stand fully undressed in the mirror, put a licked finger in her navel, and lift it to her face. She'll get back into bed, put the finger in her mouth, and touch herself thinking of you. You could get used to her. You could move to Seattle. With her you could make a new homestead. Owen would like her—Owen likes everyone after a while. You could run your classes from coffee shops in Seattle. You could learn to like the rain and the gray. You could wake her up in the middle of the night and tell her that you love her and she would say, I love you too, and you would say, No really I do with all my...what word would you put in there, *heart*, no, never—it wouldn't be true.... You say to yourself, Stop—stop—just shut the fuck up—shut the fuck up—

You hear her voice.

"What?"

She pushes herself off of your chest and smiles at you. "I was saying, I knew you'd fuck me."

You reach up and touch the ends of her hair. "I'm glad you were so sure." You smile. "There was never a time capsule up here, was there?"

"No." She bends down and pecks you on the lips. "But it's true about the janitor giving me the key. Senior year I wore it on a chain around my neck. We used to come up here at night."

"So this spot has already been broken in?"

"Sure, but this is the first time I've made love here with a widower."

"It's *made love* now?"

"Made love in retrospect."

Your back is starting to hurt and a small stone is lodged

beneath your thigh. The occasional sharp ache feels good.

"After tonight," she says, "I think I have a new theory." She lies down again on your chest.

You slip your hand underneath her hair and caress the back of her neck the way you would like someone to caress yours. "I'm listening," you say to the back of her head.

"There are people who talk about themselves in the first person, people who talk about themselves in the third person, and people who don't talk about themselves at all. Naturally you're in that last category."

"Nice theory," you say, "but my mother always taught me it's impolite to bring the conversation back around to oneself."

"Really?"

"No, but it's pretty to think so."

There's no response to the Hemingway reference, which reminds you that although she enjoyed reading, your wife either never noticed your allusions or didn't care to.

"Isn't sex bizarre?" she says.

"Only when you talk about it."

"I mean *the gotta have it*," she says, "and then when it's over, the *I can't believe I had to have it*—we're so animalistic."

"Sometimes I think animals are more like humans than humans are."

"I don't follow."

"Humans can be mean for no reason. Animals always have a reason."

"Like hunting?"

"Like sex."

On the back of her neck you feel a raised mole, which you try not to touch. She traces an eight on your thigh over and over. Even your son has figured this out—you can never caress yourself like another person can. One afternoon recently you and he were playing the body part-kissing game: *Here's a kiss on your cheek, Here's a kiss on your hand, etc.* He tried to give himself a kiss on his arm and was unsatisfied, sticking it out toward you for your lips.

Raina asks if she reminds you of your wife.

She reminds you nothing of your wife, though this is neither good nor bad. Now that you think about it, your wife never reminded you of anyone else. You should tell her that.

"It was a stupid question," she says.

"No," you say. "Everything reminds me of her." It's the same feeble answer you gave The Professor when he asked last month. *Like that walk-in closet of her clothes?* he said. *Everything,* you said. *I see, how terrible of me—it's him, he reminds you of her,* he said, *The older he gets, the more he looks like her. But not just him,* you said. *Everything—even that glass you're drinking out of. I remember picking those out because they were made in China and she always wanted to go there.* You must have been drunk. *Everything's made in China,* he said. *You see my trouble,* you said. The Professor smiled thinking it was a joke. But it wasn't. Ever since her oldest sister had gone to Shanghai on vacation (*Shanghai is the new New York! Shanghai is home to China's richest person—a woman! Shanghai has blind people who give incredible pedicures for $3!*), your wife wanted to go. And you promised to take her someday, even taking the trouble to renew her passport and get one for Owen.

Raina changes the subject: "I wish I could have seen your face after I jumped."

"Me too."

She turns her head up at you, "You know, you're more handsome without glasses."

"Thanks," you say, "I guess we should find them."

Both of you get up and rearrange your clothing. When you lift her jacket, something shiny falls out. You pick up the money clip and hold it in front of her face, "What's this?"

"Did you miss it?" she says.

"Weren't you at the auction?"

"For a little while," she says, "but it was all junk."

"The TV…" you begin, but then don't feel like getting into it.

"I saw that huge thing," she says. "What a waste of resources."

"And the clip?"

"I'm not really a pickpocket, but I'm not sorry either. I wanted to see you again."

"You thought this would do it?"

She takes the clip from you. "Just looking out for your best interests."

"What do you care?" By this point it's difficult to hide the anger. She's a fake suicide artist, widower-fucker, and thief. What's next—transexual?

"I know how you feel," she says.

"Excuse me?"

"I had a fiancée once. He drowned."

There's a distended pause. What are you supposed to say, *Sorry for your loss?*

"Engaged doesn't equal marriage," she says, "I know that."

Oh what a relief, you want to say. She sits down with her knees to her chest, arms around them, still holding the clip.

"I'm not trying to compare," she says. "But I remember how—"

"No," you say, "no more memories, no more flashbacks."

She unloosens her arms and looks up at you. She seems to notice you're upset now, and this actually makes you feel better. Calm down, you think, just get yourself out of this. "It's all right," you say, "the money clip isn't mine anyway."

"It is fake money," she says.

"I wish it were real money," you say. "Just tell me this, did you fuck me so that you could commiserate?"

"I fucked you because I wanted to."

"Because I don't want to commiserate."

"I fucked you because I wanted to."

You offer your hand and pull her up. After a couple of tries, you're able to boost her back up to the highest part of the roof. Then you climb up. It doesn't take long to find your glasses. They are intact, though you worry about possible scratches on the lens.

"I hate to say this," she says, "I have to go. I promised Beth—my friend Beth, you know, the girl who slipped on a pat of butter in the commons. Broke her hip and was on crutches for the last three months of senior year."

You have no idea what she's talking about.

"Well, I said I'd see her at the Irish pub—some people are meeting up there…." She keeps talking but you're no longer listening. You're trying to determine if she is looking up and to the left, a sign—The Professor once instructed you—that someone is making things up. She is looking up, but wait—if she's left-handed and lying, then she'll look to the right.

She interrupts your thoughts: "Do you want to come with me?"

"No, I think I'll stay up here a little longer. You know, process the evening, contemplate nonexistence, etc."

"You won't be lonely?"

"I don't understand the concept," you say. "People who get lonely must have no imagination. I feel sad for them."

"I never thought of it like that."

You wonder if you were looking up and to the left. What if you were to look up and to the left on purpose—would you be more inclined to lie if someone asked you a question?

Looking down and to the right, you say, "I'm meeting some people later, too."

"Walk me to the door?"

The whole looking this or that way seems ridiculous.

"My parents moved to Florida years ago," she says, "I won't be back here for a long time." She puts the key to the roof in your hand. Then she turns your hand over and writes her number or email, presumably—it's difficult to tell in the dark. You notice she's left-handed.

She twirls her dirty blonde hair with one hand and then kisses you on the mouth. It is a deep kiss bordering on lewd; you wonder if that is a better indication than anything else that she's telling the truth. She opens the door to the stairwell and waves goodbye.

You walk back and jump down to the spot where you made love. As in a crime scene, you replay the whole thing complete with hip thrusts—you want to be able to picture this clearly the next time you masturbate. At some point you realize you never got to see her breasts naked except for a nipple. When you get to the part where she tells you about her dead fiancée, you distinctly recall that she was looking up, dead center, at you.

11.

You push open the field house doors and head down the hill to the track. If Alex were here you'd challenge him to a race. One lap around the quarter-mile track, winner takes all. Whatever "all" might be.

At the bottom of the hill, near the starting line, you pull off your shoes, pants, and dress shirt, setting them down in a neat pile on the grass. No one is around, and what if they were? A middle-aged, slightly flabby guy in his boxers and t-shirt bending over in the set position in Lane 2, which you always preferred over the inside lane so that you could keep an eye on the favorite. You get down on all fours and take a few deep breaths.

Three, two, one—

The first hundred meters is exhilarating—wind at your back, cobalt-black darkness in front of you. Just as you were taught years ago, you extend and pump the arms fully, and the knees and legs follow in one fluid motion.

Then you hit the second hundred meters. You're sucking air harder and your right side twists—stitch cramp. Nothing to do but work through it. Your one fluid motion collapses as you feel your penis banging around in your boxers. Stupid one-eye and its demands. You should have just let Raina gone down on you, or you should have just gone down on her—you could have cried on her vulva. Or on her blouse afterwards. There should have been some crying in there, somewhere. Like in the movies. Your wife. You try to picture the last time you two made love. The weekend before she died? Two weekends before? The more you can't figure it out, can't see her on top of you or vice-versa, the more you have to figure it out. From your wife, your mind makes the small leap to Little Ma. The mother of the mother of your child. The last woman you kissed. The mother-in-law kiss. The funeral—organized by Little Ma and sisters-in-law. The only time you've been out of control in a year, and you vowed it would never happen again. Aside from crying for half an hour in the shower to no avail, the part you remember clearly was the ritual dirt-throwing on the coffin. Everyone else had taken a turn. You knew that as soon as you picked up and threw your dry clod, she would really be gone. In a moment of weakness, you muttered something to Little Ma about wanting somebody to blame beside yourself. "I don't know who you're supposed to blame," Little Ma said, "yes, you lost your wife—but I lost my best friend!" With deliberate calm, you leaned over and whispered to her, "You were supposed to die first." Father-in-law could hear, but he just sat there in his chair, head in hands, as in a movie depicting another movie—flickering and stuttering and out of focus. There was a disoriented moment. Then, with all of her eighty-nine pounds, Little Ma slapped you and it felt harder than you thought possible—and you laughed and you laughed some more and she simply stared at you—and you knew what to do then, didn't you?—you said softly, "Do it again—slap me because I deserve it"—and her remaining two daughters were there too—but you didn't want either of them—your wife was the best of the lot—Little Ma told you so once when she thought she was on her final deathbed though she wouldn't admit it later, even privately—and when Little Ma wouldn't slap you again, what did you say?—there wasn't a fucking word in the world—you grabbed her face with both hands—and you kissed her on the lips—smashing them—and you kissed her again—and there were tits and stars—and father-in-law's stuttering—and a knee to the groin—and like a blossom the pain shot up and it was full and good, it was a beginning you thought—and you re-kissed her—and because that was the closest you'll ever get again to the mouth of your wife—you kissed her again and—again and—again and—again and—again—until—you broke the seal.

You hit the finish line and everything spins. You take air in and out so fast your head feels like it's going to pop off. It does: you vomit. You bend over as far as possible. But it's too late. Warm and wet, whatever was in your stomach is now on your feet and legs. "I'm sorry," you say aloud to the god you do and do not believe in, "I'm sorry."

It finally ends but you feel no better. You walk out to the middle of the football field and lie down on your back. The grass is cool and warm at the same time. You can make out a handful of stars, though you don't see the big or little dipper—the only stars whose names you know. It's not the stars anyway that impress you—it's the expanse of blackness. You feel like an insect pinned to a velvet mat.

When you wake up it feels as though someone is standing on your chest. Everything is a muddy blur and your head pounds. Although getting any focus is exceedingly difficult, you perceive a large dark figure standing over you. You always knew the afterlife would be like this—dark and shadowy, not all whipped cream white and gold lamé. Then the figure motions with its arms.

"God?"

The arms come closer to you.

"Brother, are you all right down there?"

You know this voice.

"George?"

"Here," the voice says, handing you your glasses, "I found these on the track, along with your clothes."

It is George, and the next thing you know, he's helping you up and brushing you off. He says everyone is long gone and he's been looking for you for hours. Then he wants to know if you got lucky with that dirty blonde.

"You don't see her around, do you?" You say it more emphatically than necessary, and then add, "I got unlucky."

"She definitely was a fox."

"Yes," you say, picking grass out of your hair, "yes, she was."

"How'd you get dog shit on your legs?" he asks.

"That's not dog shit."

The two of you walk in silence across the field and up the hill. At the top, George says, "I guess not everyone left."

You look up from your grass-stained shoes, and the scene just seems too convenient: It's Jake Jones with two of his buddies—Tony McDougal, star basketball player and now star salesman, and some idiot who appears to be carrying a tire iron.

"Before we get into this," George says, "tell me what you did."

"Just don't say anything."

Maybe if you walk on by and don't even look their way....

"Hey dick-munch!"

"Dick-munch?" George says, and laughs.

"Old nickname."

They're about thirty feet away. You could run for it, but George's three hundred pounds would never make it.

"What do you want, fuck-face?" George yells and it echoes off the side of the building.

"Who's this clown?" Tony says.

About twenty feet from impact, George stops and holds out his arm preventing you from going any farther.

"This clown," George says, "is the brother-in-law. What's it to you?"

You feel as though you're watching an after school special on TV. Do they still exist?

Unknown henchman swings the tire iron around and you swear you can feel the breeze. Getting cracked with the tire iron wouldn't feel very good, but would it be totally without reward?

Jake says, "I heard you've been with my wife."

"Yeah," Tony says, "we know you poked her."

"With what," you say, "a toilet roll, a piece of licorice?"

"Funny man," henchman says.

More calmly than you expect, Jake says, "I'd simply like to know what you and her did together."

You wonder about his grammar: Shouldn't it be you and she or she and you?

Everyone is standing there, waiting for you to say something.

"What does it matter what we did fifteen years ago?"

"No, sir," Jake says. "Last night—what did you do last night?"

"Last night I didn't do anything with her. I didn't even talk to her. But fifteen years ago I may have diddled her whatchamacallit."

George laughs.

"Pound him," henchman says, "or I will."

What kind of a tool is this guy?

"I heard he's a perv too," Tony says, "internet porn dealer for little girls."

Jake looks at Tony almost annoyed.

"He teaches high school, asshole," George says.

"No one's talking to you, lard ass."

You notice that Jake's blond hair is feathered and parted in the middle exactly as it was in high school. He's still good looking of course, but you wouldn't do him were you a woman. He's too conventional, too stiff, and his grammar is bad.

"I don't care about whatever else you do," Jake says, "but I saw you with Kelly tonight."

"Well," you say, "if you say you saw us, I guess you did, but I don't remember it. Go ahead, swing away, Mr. Jones." For a second you think about closing your eyes, for fear of flinching, but the blow is already coming.

Suddenly you're on the ground and there's a lot of yelling. Your knee feels scraped raw and you've twisted your ankle, but you've not taken the blow.

Then Jake is on the ground, too, facing you. George is sitting on him.

Something very sharp is poking your thigh. You reach down and pull the button out of your pocket. "See this motherfucker," you say, pointing *Happy Birthday, Scratch!* in Jake's face.

He grunts, probably can't get a word out with George on top of him.

"I could take out your eye."

Another grunt.

"But I won't. Why, you ask? Because I've never even seen your wife's panties—not tonight, not fifteen years ago. Had I a dog in this hunt, I'd stick you with this."

You sound like a complete jackass and as this sinks in, suddenly you're aware of what's actually happening. You're lying on the ground, for no reason now, and Tony and the other guy are standing off to one side.

When you get up on your knees and back up to take in the scene, you see George threatening Jake's ass with a knife. The image is farcical, but it's obviously got them worried.

"All right, fuck-faces," George says, "time for you to walk to your cars nicely and drive the fuck away."

You get to your feet, twisted ankle and all, but you don't really know what to do. Hold the button out at them like a shank? Say something threatening? It doesn't matter. The two men take one more look at George and the knife, which must be six inches long, and then they head off.

"We'll be back," one of them says, and then adds, "cock-suckers."

Once they've turned the corner of the building, you tell George to get off him.

"Once more sec." He raises himself up a few inches and lets out a tremendous fart.

Jake rolls out from underneath George and takes off.

George is laughing so hard he's bent over. "Did you...did you..." He can't finish the sentence.

"What is that thing, a hunting knife?"

"It's dull," he says. "It's huge but it's dull. I don't think I could've cut through the shit in his pants."

"How did you know they were coming after me?"

"Never mind," he says, and pulls up his left pant leg. He slips the knife into a holster. "You're my wife's brother, I look out for kin."

"Who are you, Daniel fucking Boone? I'm not your kin. Shit, my sister isn't even technically my kin."

"Fuck you," he says.

"Why'd you come here tonight anyway? If you wanted to

feel better about yourself, you could've gone down to the town pump and sat at the bar and watched how bad life can get."

"That's fucking low," he says. "I only do that once a year, to see how those sorry asses drink down their Christmas dinner."

"It's fucked."

"So what—it always makes me feel better."

You start for the parking lot. Your ankle is killing you. He follows like some kind of stupid dog.

"I'm not a hard case, and I don't need your guardian angelship. You should have let them kick the shit out of me."

"That would've been too easy," he laughs, "I'll do it myself someday."

He catches up to you and tries to put his arm around you, but you push it away.

"Owen's my only kin."

"Your wife—"

He tries to put his arm on you again, and you wheel around with your fist. The punch lands on the side of his neck.

"Jesus," he says and rubs his neck. He doesn't want to hit you—you can see that. You throw another with your left hand and this one does it—smack in his jaw.

When you come to, you see a charcoal-pink sheet of sky. You're lying on a strip of grass between parking spots. Your head hurts and you feel a lump on your right temple. When you finally get up, your ankle gives out. Leaning against your parents' car, you take an awkward piss. On the windshield of the car is a note: *Cheap shot, dick-munch.*

It's after four a.m. when you pull into your parents' driveway. The house is dark except for the stovetop light. Mom hasn't waited up for you this time.

You go upstairs to the bathroom, run warm water over your

hands and wash your face, and then go sit on the floor next to the
bed where Owen is sound asleep.

"I've never told you this," you begin. "Your grandma isn't
your real grandma. What I mean is that she is and she isn't.
What I mean is—well, you and me we share something special.
A little fucked up special, but special. I know, mommy wouldn't
approve of the swearing. That's what I'm trying to get across:
My biological mom and your biological mom—they're both
gone. We can swear if we want to. Mine went MIA years ago,
and yours, I guess you could say, died in combat. Don't lecture
me about the metaphor, okay. Now if my bio mom is alive,
she'd be seventy-one this year. Yes, that's pretty fucking old,
especially in toddler years. Yours? Yes, you're right, she'd be
thirty-one. But look at the mode of that sentence. I know you're
not familiar with it. It's the conditional. The point is that neither of our bio moms is with us. They never will be. What does
that mean in an everyday way, outside of the conditional? Good
question. Anyway, your grandma—the one who raised me in
this house—she's your grandma, she *is* my mother of course.
I love her. How could I not? So I have two mothers, which is
extra special. The problem is that I can't seem to help either of
them. The one here—you know something about that. And the
one who shot me out her vagina—she's out there somewhere
and I just don't understand how she could be happy not knowing
me, how I turned out—not that I'm any great shakes—what's
that supposed to mean 'shakes'—Shakespeare? Not that I'm any
great Shakespeare. Well…let me put it this way, I can't imagine what life would be like without you in it—yes, you, Owen
Douglas—and so I *can* imagine what she is missing. If she has any
imagination at all, then some part of her, even a small part, is
sad. Profoundly sad. And so some part of me is sad too. I know,
it's tiresome. I'll let you rest now."

You kiss him on the head. He rustles and moans a little. You hope he's dreaming of lambs, kitties, or large breasts.

"You are a sweet, sweet boy. More precious to me than...." The words get choked off. The tears are coming but you stop them, as if they would admit that your love beyond reason for your son is unoriginal.

12.

Sometimes you wake up and think she is there next to you. On the mornings you wake up and do not think she is next to you, like this morning, you still think of her lying in bed. You cannot imagine a morning when you shall wake up and not think about her or the absence of her next to you. When you told this to The Professor at breakfast one morning, he said: "Don't think about her—the more you think about her, the less honest your memory of her will become."

You told him you didn't need his professional opinion today and that you would think about her whenever you goddamn felt like it or didn't feel like it.

"But each memory is an action of creation," he said. "When you have a memory, specific cells in your brain recreate the event—in the same chemical reactions and in the same physical locations of the brain as when you first made the memory. The recreation, however, isn't exact—it gets subtly altered each time, which means the more you have that memory, the more it's subject to change and therefore the less reliable it is to the first experience of it."

You would like to have told him to fuck himself with his ex-wife's corncob dildo. But you knew he was trying to help, in his overbearing way, so instead you said: "You're telling me then that the most honest memory of her is the one I don't think about very often."

"Precisely. If you keep running over in your mind, say, the first time you kissed your wife, you're altering that memory slightly each time so that by a certain point, the memory could theoretically be much different than the actual event."

"I shouldn't think of my wife?"

"If you want the most honest memory of her to remain in tact—yes, that's what I'm saying."

"That's crazy."

"That's science."

You pull yourself up from the carpet, which you have mistakenly thought was a bed. You look down at your wristwatch. It's almost ten o'clock.

Where is your son?

Then you register the distant sound of pots and pans banging. On weak ankle and with throbbing head, you make it downstairs to find your mother making French toast for Owen, who is at her feet with metal spatula in hand. He sees you and goes back to banging.

"Morning."

"You must have been tired."

"I usually get up with him around 6:30."

"That's okay. We've been having a grand time down here. Owen helped me fold laundry this morning, didn't you?" She bends down and presses his nose like a button.

You sit at the kitchen table with a cup of coffee. After a while you hear Dad's steps on the stairs, the familiar crack of his shins. You've heard that crack thousands of times, noticed it in your own legs at home when you try to make it down the stairs as quietly as possible after putting Owen down for a nap.

At breakfast Owen eats a whole piece of French toast by himself, even before you've taken a bite.

Dad seems to be enjoying his as well, despite being told by Mom, "Nobody's going to take that away from you, Michael."

You move on to a second cup of coffee.

"We're going to church this morning," Mom says. "Would you and Owen like to join us?"

Church? She must be kidding. They stopped going to church—his Catholic, hers Protestant—ages ago, 1986 to be exact. And even before that the record is spotty, though sometimes they dragged you and your sister to both mass and service, one after the other.

You set Owen down on the floor and he takes off into the family room. Because you say "Be careful of the fireplace," it's the first place he heads. You chase after him. He trips on the shag carpet and knocks his head on the wall. It makes a loud noise but obviously hasn't hurt him. He gets up a little dizzily and looks like a mini Buster Keaton. He sees you laugh. And so he purposefully knocks his head on the wall again and falls down. For a moment it's funny and you're happy that he's trying to please you. After the third time, you worry that he's not trying to please you, he's trying to put himself out of his misery.

You bring him back to the kitchen table and let him play with some raisins, which you cut in half.

"I don't think Owen would make it through service."

"Suit yourself."

Suit yourself? Does she really want to deal with a toddler ripping pages from the hymnal and climbing around in the pews?

Owen has thrown a few half-raisins over the side of the table. One of the cats is knocking one around on the floor. This amuses him so he tosses over the rest.

"Nice one," you say and give him a kiss.

You finish breakfast and start clearing dishes.

Mom starts talking about the family reunion they went to a few weeks ago. "It was hot and humid. I would have voted for another weekend later in the season, but it wasn't for me to say. It was a good turnout. Your father's brothers paid for the pavilion rental, the chicken, and the Italian beef and rolls. We brought potato salad and a tray of brownies."

"Didn't you think something was wrong with the beef?" Dad says.

"I don't know," she says, "didn't taste funny to me."

"I think it was bad."

"My least favorite sister-in-law, Ellen," Mom continues, "brought cookies but kept them for her family and wouldn't share with the rest of us. But she is fast to grab more than her share of leftover desserts to take on home for her and Dennis to have afterward. Jessica had some boyfriend there, bald and with a big grey mustache—I don't like those things but to eat his own."

To eat his own. Classic. You'd forgotten about that one. It's funny until you realize how much this stuff occupies the space of her mind and, thus, your conversations.

Somehow the conversation segues into politics.

"I wonder about your father's brothers," Mom says, "if they'd vote for a black man."

"What do you think, Dad?"

He doesn't respond. Not because the question upsets him, but because he hasn't heard the question. You repeat it.

"I don't know," he says, "I think Bob would."

Before Mom and Dad leave for church, she asks you to make a list of Christmas gift ideas for Owen. Sure, you say, not knowing that you'll get to the airport later, get through security, and then remember you never wrote it.

After they leave, you try to keep Owen from pulling down every book and bauble in the house. Finally you take him to the park down the street. When you were a kid, it was a field of scrub oak and weeds. Now there's manicured greenery and an enormous jungle gym. You watch him climb and run around, occasionally getting up to prevent the eating of a pebble or the handling of a sharp stick.

It's hard to make the idyllic image in front of you coincide with the one of your childhood. It's always been a nice, safe subdivision except for one incident. When you were around ten, a girl about your age was stabbed. She'd been walking by herself early evening on the sidewalk where the park is now. The assailant ran into the woods and soon neighborhood fathers were dispatched. They searched all night but never found him. The girl and her family moved away a few months later. You're so invested in figuring out whether your dad was one of the paternal posse that you don't see Owen climbing the big boy slide until it's too late.

He falls off and nails his elbow on the turf. His mouth opens as wide as possible and it takes a few seconds for the wailing to begin. You hold him and sing the first song you ever sang for him: *Michael Row Your Boat Ashore.* But you do the version where you change Michael to Owen. After a few rounds he calms down enough for you to head back home.

Owen is having a snack and you're on the third cup of coffee when Mom and Dad return. Dad is pleased: He has bought corn on the cob, six for a dollar, and a bag full of apples at a Mexican fruit stand.

Owen starts to unpack the bags on the kitchen floor. Not only does he often enjoy this, but he's actually helpful.

Dad goes into the family room and turns on the TV. It's so

loud that when he comes back into the kitchen the sound of the TV is not in background but in the foreground. He says, "Dominick's is going out of business and it serves them right."

"I like Dominick's," you say, "or used to—I remember going there as a kid, especially after church in Crystal Lake. You and Mom would sometimes splurge and get us doughnuts."

"But now they try to cheat you."

"What?"

"They advertise lettuce at 99 cents a head and then charge you $1.29 at the checkout. You have to watch those guys."

You decide not to argue with him.

"Our flight's at two," you say. "I'm sorry we won't be able to eat the corn-on-cob with you."

"That's okay," he says. "Here, have an apple."

You take a bite. It's mealy but you say, "Good apple." Owen loves apples so you give it to him. "Give grandpa a kiss, O." He dutifully makes a pucker sound.

Dad smiles and takes out two more apples. "For your trip," he says, and washes them in the sink where the faucet has been wrapped in ten feet of electrical tape to prevent leaks.

"We'll have to leave in an hour," you say.

"I didn't realize," Mom says, entering the kitchen.

"I thought I mentioned it."

"You didn't," she says, and then softens her tone, "are you going to be back for Thanksgiving?"

"I'm not sure yet."

"Your Aunt Hilda will come in that morning, of course. She'd love to see you and Owen."

"We'll try."

You reach down to pet Owen's head but he's not there. You find him around the corner sitting next to the cat food bowls, and in the nick of time you stop his hand from putting a triangle-shaped kibble in his mouth. "Nice one, O," you say. With his free hand he immediately reaches for another kibble—this one x-shaped. "Owen Douglas, you know better."

"You little stinker," Mom says. First you think she's talking about Owen but then you realize Asia, the cat you've not seen all weekend, is rubbing up against Mom's leg.

"Look at all these bowls, O—seven!" you say. "That's one lucky cat."

Mom picks up Asia and holds her like a baby, rubbing her ears. "I don't know why your father provides a smorgasbord for little Asia," Mom says. "Michael, come over here and pick up some of these bowls."

Owen turns over one of them, sending kibbles in all directions.

"Daddy's little helper," Mom says. "This cat reminds me of the first cat I had as a girl on the farm. Snow had this beautiful white coat." She sits down at the kitchen table, Asia still pressed against her. You show Owen how to pick up each kibble and put it back into the bowl.

"Snow's mother died in birth," Mom says, "so I fed her with a bottle. Then Snow herself lost her litter, kicked by a cow, but she adopted Marble's—that was our pet duck—ducklings. She'd bathe them, carry them around like they were her own kittens. Asia's more finicky in the eating department, of course, but she's a sweet thing."

Dad picks up one of the bowls but sets down a new one. Mom doesn't notice. "The car needs gas," he says, "we'd better leave a little early."

Dad asks you to drive, which he often does when you're in town. He has always thought you're the safest driver (your sister the worst, your mother somewhere in between); he probably won't grab the dashboard more than two or three times in anticipation of the car braking.

You strap Owen into his car seat and your mother begins reading him a book. It's another of his favorites which you lug around everywhere, a permanent item in the diaper bag. The story of the baby water buffalo who is afraid to take a bath almost never fails to enchant him. Mom gets to the part where the baby water buffalo is about to run away from home, and you remember how soothing her reading voice is. She always inhabited the characters' voices distinctively and knew where the right cadences and inflections should be—a skill you hope to master by the time Owen can actually comprehend stories.

You've made this drive from Algonquin to O'Hare numerous times, and it is an uneventful ride until you approach a toll-booth. You ask Dad for the electronic I-PASS.

"I couldn't find it last time I needed it," he says, and gestures across the dashboard, "just get in the 'cash only' lane."

"What do you mean you couldn't find it?" Mom says.

You try to prevent a possible argument by reminding him that the I-PASS can be attached to the windshield with velcro.

"No," Dad says, "someone would steal it."

"What?"

"I saw it in the news, they smash your windshield and take it."

"Who?"

"Whoever. I usually keep it under the seat but it's not there. You'd better change lanes—get over, get over."

You cut across three lanes of traffic, Dad gripping the dashboard and simultaneously searching the glove compartment for change. You unintentionally cut off a sports car, whose driver gives you the finger, which normally might irritate you, but you simply smile and wave at him.

Dad hands you a sticky dime. "Martha—" he says. But she is

already riffling through her purse the size of a backpack.

"Where's all my damn change?" she says.

Oh shit, Dad's scribblings and the photocopying.

"It's gone," you say.

"What do you mean *it's gone?*"

"You know, Mom, Friday night...I...used it...."

"What do you mean *you used it?*"

You can't believe how dense she is being.

"Don't go into my things," she scolds, pulling items out one after another as if in a cartoon.

"Jesus, you know why I was in there."

She keeps muttering on about not going into her things. Your father doesn't seem to notice the rising voices, having been through these strange exercises too many times over the course of a long marriage.

"We still need another eighty cents," you say.

Because you've been too busy defending your position in pilfering all of her change, you haven't noticed that you're still a lane away from the "manual" lane and it's too late to get over.

When you pull up alongside the tollbooth, it is unmanned—there's only the change receptacle—so you wait. Your father now is busy with his hands underneath the seats, turning up old coffee cups, dried-up banana peels, an empty bottle of odorless garlic pills, and various scraps of paper which you suspect are filled with more missives about Atlantis. You were stupid not to have simply taken the originals.

Owen appears to take all the fuss in stride. He's eating his Cheerios like popcorn, watching everyone tear up the car.

The cars behind you start laying on the horn. You put the car in park, and turn around to the backseat.

"What would you like me to do, Mother?"

"I don't like it when people go into my things," she says, and makes a face.

The honking has grown to an absurd level. You've always found Midwesterners to be friendly folks, but now someone has rolled down his window and is tossing out expletives. You notice a tollbooth worker on her way over.

"All right, all right," says Dad.

Mother keeps talking about how you've violated her privacy, her *things*.

"All right already!" Dad yells and slams down his hand on the dashboard. You wonder what they saw in each other all those years ago. If Mom would have married Dad had she known about the schizophrenia in advance. If Dad would have married Mom had he known about the schizophrenia in advance. If Mom would have married Dad had she known she'd have to nag him ceaselessly about splashing shaving water around the bathroom sink. If Dad would have married Mom had he known she didn't like men with facial hair....

The tollbooth person knocks on your window. She is bundled up in a sweater and jacket, even though it must be sixty degrees out. She yells at the window, "What's the trouble here?"

You don't turn around but you do offer her a raised index finger, the same way you do for Owen and say *one minute* when you're in the middle of something.

"No change," she yells. "Do you have a bill?"

With Mom still ranting about her change, Dad gets out his wallet, takes out a five, and hands it out to you.

You could easily take the bill. But you can't stand this scene, the feelings of pity you have for your parents and the absurdity of the coins. Significance rubbing up against triviality. Then an idea: *Run the toll.* Your father's paranoia and your mother's carping. *Just run the damn thing.* Hundreds of shards of wood everywhere. *Run it.* It'll be glorious. *Now.* You turn once more around to your mother, give her steady look, turn back again, and with both hands on the wheel, you slam your foot on the gas.

The engine roars and screeches.

But the car doesn't move. You've forgotten to take it out of park.

After a moment, you take the five dollars, roll down the window, and mumble an apology. Without a word, the woman hands you change and releases the gate.

"What were you thinking?" Dad says, looking back.

You don't really know. It seemed like an excessive, but not a truly violent, action. You expect Dad to go on, to chew you out for gunning the engine, ruining the transmission or something, but he doesn't. Mom says nothing. The airport is only fifteen minutes away now.

Light traffic on a Sunday morning. Periodically scanning on-ramps for police cars, you continue barreling down the highway in silence. In the rearview mirror, you can see Owen playing with his Cheerios.

The silence grows and becomes unbearable. It suddenly seems fitting that your mind is cast back one more time to a similar silence. You were sitting in the backseat of your parents' car, which was parked in front of the security gate at Northrop. You were still wearing your track sweats. Mom had gone inside to collect him. You waited and waited and then, for some reason, he came out alone. His hair was perfectly combed and slicked back and his tie was securely fastened in its usual double-Windsor knot. He opened the car door and sat down in the passenger's seat. He didn't say anything and you didn't know what to say. You sat there behind him waiting. The silence grew with the lump in your throat. At some point, he turned his head slowly so that you could see his profile. The rest of his body remained rigid, facing forward. You could see his left eye swell, about to capsize. You had never seen him cry, not even at his own father's funeral, and now it was particularly unsettling because his left eye was his wandering eye. Then he said, "I'm sorry, I didn't mean to fail you and Elizabeth." It is either the closest or the farthest you have ever felt to him, and the only thing you finally managed to reply was, "I know, Dad, I know."

You miss the exit for "Departures" but no one says anything. When you get in the lane for U-turns, Mom says, "Park in the garage, we'll walk you in."

All the times you've come to visit over the years, they always drop you off at the curb. What must've gone through Dad's head when he's come out to the airport with you each time. All your past girlfriends who've visited with you, all the different places you've gone to and come back from. Is he glad he doesn't have to fly? Does he want to take a trip? The handful of times he's mentioned to you wanting to see Paris and the Eiffel Tower. Do you want him to envy you because you've seen Paris, many times, and traveled much farther? If he does envy you, then he's done his job as a father. If he doesn't envy you, then he's failed. Isn't that how you're going to measure your worth as Owen's father?

"We'd love to see you at Thanksgiving," Mom says, and sets down your suitcase.

Dad has gone to get your boarding passes from the automatic check-in.

"We'll try," you say, "though my in-laws already invited us to New York." It's a lie, but it'll give you an out later if you want it.

You try to hand Owen to your mother for a goodbye hug. He doesn't want to—he's notoriously awful at goodbyes—so you put him down and hold on to his hand.

When you embrace her, she says "I'm sorry" into your ear. Is she apologizing about what happened in the car? Normally she'd sulk about something like that for a couple of weeks. You suddenly have a terrible and ridiculous feeling you will never see her again. At first it's as if someone else is holding on to to your mother, clenching his eyes tight, trying to fix the moment in his mind. And then something hits the gut, the throat, and the entire chest—your whole body shakes. People must be watching and thinking what a melodramatic fraud you are. But there's no escaping it—if your mind doesn't recognize this, your body does. She is shorter than you by a head but that doesn't stop you from crying hard into her shoulder. You've only done this one other time—as a teenager, post-father-schizophrenia-discovery, after smashing a pear into the kitchen floor, and then saying *I hate money, I hate money* over and over until she held you and the crying jag ran its course. Now your mind keeps repeating what your mouth won't say: *I'm sorry I can't help you, I'm sorry I can't help you.*

You finally peel yourself from her and notice that Owen is clutching your leg. You pick him up and press his face against yours, to hide any residual tears. Owen is always good in this way—he knows you need the embrace more than he does. He hugs and kisses you because you need it, not because he wants it. That is his job, a son's job, in this world. Then you feel something else—you feel your wife's cheek against yours. That smooth, flawless cheek you used to press up against— you should have counted how many times, it would mean something to know exactly how many times you pressed and kissed each other, you could use that—that number—you could build something with it, play the lottery with it, tattoo it on to your chest. Then it hits you—the last time you and she pressed and kissed. It wasn't full intercourse, just 69. She rubbed her lips against the tip of your penis. Something she rarely did. Something you regularly wanted her to do but were too embarrassed to ask for. One of her hands around your waist and the other on your torso. The tip and her hands and the tip turning into the shaft and the shaft turning into the testicles and the testicles turning into the anus and after that you lost track—until the screaming came from down the hall. It wasn't the first time the little man interrupted your once-a-week, Saturday afternoon make-out sessions, and were you to know that it would be the last, you would have fucked your wife with every fiber—present, past, future—carried her into every room, on top and below every piece of furniture, through every opening and crevice—three or four or five times—until—until—until—the baby screamed his lungs bloody and raw.

You raise your head slowly. Owen is red-faced, tight-eyed, and sniffling. Mom is patting his back, "It's okay, Daddy's okay," she keeps saying. You look over and see that your father's eyes are wet. At least you've given him that.

The moment is broken by the smell of fresh excrement; Owen has soiled himself.

You say goodbye to your parents one last time, without words. You wave and hold Owen.

In the men's room you discover he has a bad case of diaper rash. Searching for the special triple-cream ointment your wife used to buy, you find a lot of junk in the baby bag, including the unread novel. Might as well let Owen air out diaper-less for a minute.

You're about to open the book, when Owen grabs it from you.

"All right," you say, "I'll ask a question and you open the book and read us the answer."

He nods.

"What now?" you ask.

He nods again.

"What now, honey?"

He nods. You help him open the book to a random page, and read: "…and so it was over, again. He lay in bed for three days, tasting the residue of her voice in his throat as if…." You toss the book in the garbage. It lands in wads of wet paper towels, not even making a thud.

13.

First you think it's your ears, wax build-up or a stress-triggered migraine. Then you realize it's intermittent. Your cell phone is ringing. It could be your sister—or worse George. Then again it might be Alex Mueller.

You dig it out of the baby bag. The number isn't familiar.

"Hello?"

"Hi, it's Raina."

"Hi."

"What are you doing right now?"

"I'm at O'Hare."

"I'd like to see you."

"I'm at the airport."

The other end seems to go dead.

"Hello, hello?"

"I'm here," she says.

Owen starts to stand up in his stroller. He's looking at a police dog. "Sit down," you say, pushing him back down. You wonder if the police dog has tracked you down because of the fight in the parking lot, the tollbooth incident, or simply because you feel guilty for being alive. "Ruff, ruff," Owen says, and sticks out his tongue and pants.

"What?"

"Not you."

"I'm sorry, it's Owen. I'm at the airport."

"Owen?"

"My son."

"I didn't know his name."

"Owen—after John Irving's Owen Meany."

"Who?"

"Never mind," you say. "Look, I'll send you an email."

"I need to tell you something right now. What I didn't get to finish last night."

"Last night is finished," you say, and then regret it.

"Okay."

"That came out wrong."

Owen has gotten one arm free and is trying to push himself out of the stroller again.

"Hold on," you say, putting the phone under your arm. You re-situate him and cinch down on his shoulder strap. "It's all right, honey, we're almost there." He puts on his pouty face. "What does a doggie say?" *Ruff, ruff.*

"He's fine now," you say into the phone.

"My fiancé…." she begins but then stops.

You try to be as patient as possible. The pause goes on and on. Owen begins banging his head up and down in frustration—or maybe it's the first sign of autism. Christ. "I'm sorry," you say, "but we have to go here."

"He drowned."

"Who? Oh right—yes I know."

"But I didn't tell you *why* he drowned."

The water was deep, you want to say.

"He was trying to save me, because I was the one drowning. But he drowned, he drowned." She starts crying into the phone.

You don't know what to say, and you've never known

what to say. To anyone.

She's crying into the phone. You are standing in the middle of the airport, looking at the back of your son's head which is bobbing up and down.

She's crying into the phone. His head is so goddamn beautiful, even if his hair is cut crooked in spots because you try to do it when he's sleeping. What a beautiful head.

She's crying into the phone and you bend over and kiss the most exquisite head that has ever existed and is now banging up and down furiously.

Before you know what you're doing you say, "Stop it, hon, I love you." You kiss his head, holding it still, and say it again, "Stop, I love you."

She's stopped crying. "Me too," she says.

"I have to go," you say.

"Me too."

"Goodbye."

You continue on in a daze. The airport feels extra cold, and your hands are turning to ice. What do you have to warm them? A toddler in an umbrella stroller and a photo of your wife. Reaching for your wallet in your jacket pocket, you pull out your passport, which is there only because you let your driver's license expire. And tucked inside your passport is Owen's passport.

You stop right there in the middle of the concourse and take in the simultaneity. There are business people rushing past you on a Sunday, church-like, quietly and deliberately. They are probably good people and there's no reason to make an opinion of them in order to make an opinion of yourself. And yet you often wonder why people try to be perfect like machines and machines try to be imperfect like people. These travelers connect the food courts, luggage stores, duty-free shops, restrooms,

TV lounges. In all the et cetera you spy a scene: a young woman embracing an older woman—obviously a homecoming—and right next to them another young woman trying not to sob into the arms of her boyfriend or husband or brother, who is wearing the most beautiful dress shirt you've ever seen. Then by chance or fate—it doesn't matter anymore—you smell ammonia-based floor cleaner tempered by the scent of hazelnut coffee. Nuts. More fucking nuts.

Close your eyes to all of it...

…and imagine that day, that night, that man and his infant son…

"Do you want your milky-milk?" he says, and shakes the bottle.

No response.

"You don't want your milky-milk?" he says, and shakes it with the other hand.

The city is very busy that day, right before the Christmas weekend, and the man navigates his stroller through the crowded sidewalks like a steward through a jammed ice floe. At least this is what you believe he thinks. He has agreed to let his wife have some free time, a rare occurrence, so that she and her mother can go shopping for a few hours. Instead of taking the baby to Central Park, however, like he told his wife he would do, the man decides last minute to call up an old friend. Every time he visits the city, it is a high drama of three sisters-in-law, fallout from grandparents' divorce, and grandma's relentless colon cancer. Just once he would like to visit the Guggenheim, enjoy an intimate dinner with his wife, or meet an old friend for a drink.

The man and his baby and the old friend, an investment banker, meet at Chumley's, an artists' bar which has since been torn down. It is awkward in the beginning (the two men having not seen each other in ten years) but after the first drink they are chatting away like a couple of elderly sisters. Or perhaps this is simply what the man thought at the time; you can't be sure. At one point, the old friend gets up to use the men's room. The man notices the quality of his friend's charcoal, pinstripe suit, which would cost the man a month's salary. But this does not bother the man; he doesn't want to be a banker and he doesn't want to live in this city. But to enjoy a drink or two in this spot, in this moment.... The old friend returns and begins talking about his recent visit to Cuba, a place the man has always wanted to see before it's ruined by the rest of world. The old friend talks about the wedding he attended—the rum, the cigars, the gorgeous dilapidation of it all, like some kind of Garden of Eden in Hell. The man can't quite conjure up a picture in his mind, but he enjoys trying like you do now. Soon the baby is asleep and the men fall into and then through a third pint. "Guinness," the old friend says, "they used to give it to pregnant women because of the high iron content." There is more talk and laughter, mostly about the past. There will be no future between the men and even without saying it, they are somehow aware of this now. A turn in the conversation reminds the man that he promised to make dinner for his wife and her mother.

They part ways on the sidewalk, one uptown and one downtown. The man and his baby are already late, so he will have to pick up something. There's a new Thai place on the corner, near his mother-in-law's apartment, which he has been meaning to try. He orders chicken curry for himself, soup for his ailing mother-in-law, and an extra-large papaya salad, his wife's favorite.

The man and baby arrive at the apartment just ahead of his wife and her mother. He sets the table while they bathe the baby and get him ready for sleep. A canary yellow onesie, the one with blue airplanes and orange hot-air balloons, is laid out on the bed. The man unpacks the food into bowls and plates. In bending over for a dropped spoon, he feels a sharp pain in his side. It's that same spot in his digestive tract, distended again and flaring because of stress. He knows he shouldn't have had that last drink—alcohol often aggravating the juncture between his large and small intestine. He pours down the drain the bottle of beer he has just opened.

When the baby is asleep, the man and his wife and her mother sit down for dinner. Everyone is famished. The man makes a plate of papaya salad for his wife, and she begins eating it as if it were her last meal.

It is.

At first he thinks she's choking on something—a perennial, if mundane, worry—but then she says her chin's numb and her stomach feels like it's dropped out. By the time the man and his wife have figured out that there is some kind of tree nut not normally in the salad (it will turn out later to be ground cashews), her face and throat have ballooned. Anaphylactic shock. Soon scaly hives appear on her neck and her chest tightens. The man finds the epipen in his wife's purse and jams it into her thigh, but his angle is wrong and the needle breaks clean off at the stem.

On the way to the hospital, the EMTs let the man sit in the ambulance just like he'd imagined in one of his middle-of-the-night panic attacks. But his imagination had never ridden all the way to the hospital in the ambulance. At first the ride seems to take forever but then she loses consciousness and the ride never takes long enough. The EMTs try to hold the man back because he's shaking her shoulders and yelling now: *Dammit, we're not finished! We're not finished! We're not finished.* The EMTs have seen it before, there's nothing for them to imagine. But this doesn't stop the man from yelling the words again and again until he's punched in the arm with a tranquilizer and thrown out of the way.

Then there is the window of the ambulance. He sees the cars that have pulled over. People who feel good about themselves for letting an ambulance pass. People who connect cars to cars to cars.

On the floor of the hallway the man is not crying and then he is crying; the jag is so hard that he slams his head against the wall. There is an immediate lump the size of a peach. Two medical students are concerned about a concussion, but when they try to help he screams. Neither their hands nor their imaginations can touch him.

Time passes, maybe half an hour, and the man drags himself to the bathroom.

He washes his face and examines it closely for the first time in years. Every line and contour, every dot of stubble, every pore and blemish. There is a small whitehead in the crease of his nose. With both hands, he squeezes his face hard until the pimple explodes in puss and blood...

For god's sake open your eyes and begin walking.

Drag the suitcase, push the stroller. Whether or not the man you were that night will go on blaming the man you are or will become, you cannot predict. You know one thing, however; you will never again have a drink with an old friend. There are no more old friends.

Drag the suitcase, push the stroller.

You reach the moving walkway between concourses B and C of the United terminal—the famous neon light tunnel. It's something out of the history of the future, run by three computers, someone once told you, a mile of neon penciling the ceiling with a light show that is never the same twice. The experience is so stunning and gorgeous that Owen is blinded by it and beginning to cry.

Where are you going?

Home, of course, but what's the point? She won't be there to stack the dishes in the drying rack like a house of cards, and you won't have to delicately pull out the card that is the lid to

Owen's bottle. She won't make the chocolate, corn flour waffles on Monday morning, and you won't have to pretend to like them more than the plain, store-bought waffles in the freezer. She won't have to bite her lip every time you lock the front door, even when you go downstairs only to fetch the mail. And later while you are not making love to her, you won't have to say *I love this body of yours*, and she won't reply *Don't all men say that when they're getting laid.*

Say goodbye to her. Say goodbye to *we* and *us* and *I*. Say goodbye to all the fucking nuts in the world—both human and tree.

You turn around and head in the direction you came.

It doesn't take as long as you thought to reach the international wing. You check the screens. *Son of a bitch.* The woman next to you flinches, and you sense she wants to say something like *Some people are plain crude*, something Mom would say. Owen lets out a moan and points to his face. With your sleeve you wipe his pale green nose drip. You turn back to the displays. There has got to be what you want up there. Then you realize you're looking at the arrivals. You smile and excuse yourself past the woman.

There. Departure. A flight, a number, and a time.

You are standing before a tinted window staring out at planes on the tarmac. Owen presses his nose and open mouth against the glass.

"I know," you say, "I've missed the window, so to speak, of opportunity, haven't I?"

He shakes his head, though you can't tell if it's in agreement or disgrace.

"I'm talking about suicide, of course," you say. "What, you

don't think I ever had the balls? Probably not. Yes, this will be a long flight. And yes, we could keep on catching flights one after another, until one of them crashes. But that could take months, or years. You're right about the big S word—it should be allowed. In ancient times it was heroic. You were the only one who could take your own life, no one else was worthy of doing it. Don't ask me why we've gone backwards in that department. It's all beside the point anyway."

Owen's nose and mouth have left a slobbery print on the window. He begins running his index finger through it and pointing out at the planes.

"It's so unnatural," you say, "I agree with you. I don't care how many times people have explained thrust, airflow, and lift to me—it's wrong that those things get off the ground. People aren't meant to fly, are they?"

He nods.

"Good, I like it when we agree. We don't always have to, you know, but I like it."

Then he shakes his head, as if there is a flaw in this plan.

"Okay, so we don't know a soul in Shanghai, and my rusty German won't get us very far. But you small people catch on fast with languages, you'll be fine. And it's China, honey, the next world power. I know people have been saying that since I was a baby, but maybe it will turn out to be the America of the 21st Century. I'd like to give you that, a kind of new old world. Think about it—didn't the Jews once take exile in Shanghai? I don't know, we're going to have to do some reading up."

He nods again, which you knew he would because he has always enjoyed books—the touch and heft of them, if not their words.

"Soon," you say, "we're going to walk into a world where our silence will be understood."

He fails to nod.

"What, you think we're supposed to have an undying loyalty to the utter loneliness of America? I believe it's quiet patriotic, in fact, to strike out for the West, my boy. We will go so far west it will become East."

Owen turns around and starts walking away.

"Come back here," you say. He has picked up a discarded section of a newspaper and is heading for a trashcan. "Oh, I see, you're trying to tell me that some people will think that we couldn't face facts, that we're running away, that running away is easy and for cowards. Let me simply raise the possibility that those same people never go anywhere and that is, one might argue, more like running away than running away is."

You are only a few feet behind him now but some fifty feet away from your seats; you worry that security will come destroy your unattended luggage.

He turns around before the trash can and raises his arms. He wants you to pick him up so that he can throw away the newspaper.

"Only if you take back what you implied earlier about my 'escaping' home after discovering Dad was schizo. I didn't escape, I merely went to college as planned."

He knows this linguistic charade is just to hide the fact that you barely feel like an adult even though you're pushing forty. If he could really talk, he would say three little words: *God help us.* You don't know much but you do know this: God only exists to give your son someone to believe in when you're gone.

The poor boy's arms reach up higher. "Before I lift you up," you say, "I want you to answer one last question—can a passenger also be a pilot?"

He nods vigorously, and you pick him up and squeeze him tight, crunching the newspaper between the two of you.

They make the first call for boarding. You put one foot in front of the other, dragging the suitcase behind you. Owen pushes the stroller in front of you. Teamwork.

You are the first to board coach. Rows and rows of gray seats. You try not to think of tombstones. After securing the luggage, assembling your spot, and strapping Owen into the window seat, there's nothing to do but wait. He isn't tired; he's still curious and looks out at the wing. From his seat he tries to slap at the window but can't quite reach.

Passengers file in and the flight begins to look very full. You give Owen the in-flight magazine, but he's not in the mood for tearing things apart. He's more interested in your wristwatch, so you give it to him and he tries to put it on. You hope he loses it; you've never liked wearing a watch.

Crewmembers pantomime the emergency procedures while the plane pushes back. The first officer makes some pleasant remarks as the plane taxis and then waits on the tarmac. Her voice is raspy and you imagine a pretty, middle-aged woman who wears her hair in a neat bun underneath her co-pilot's cap. You tell Owen to prepare for take-off, hold his hand, and then you close your eyes. His hand is warm and calm, yours is cool and damp. Ying-yang, yes, a perfect team. You feel the plane make a quick turn and then shoot down the runway. Even though it's ridiculous, beginning with your dead wife, you run down the list of people you love, picturing each in your mind in case this is the last time you'll ever see them.

Someday, as if all this had been carefully planned out, you will tell Owen the story of your wife. For now, it will simply have to be enough to ask for her forgiveness. Because when this plane finally lifts off, you have to let her go.